Edwards Investigations
The Rimer File

P.J. MacLayne

Dedication

In memory of my recently departed mother, Helen Louise Guth, who always supported my creative efforts, even if she didn't fully understand them. This is a story she would have found too scary to read, but would have admired anyway. She gave me the freedom to be myself, even if she didn't agree with my decisions. I miss you, Mom.

Description

The 80s. Pittsburgh, PA. A man's world.

All Annie McGregor wanted was to nail a cheating husband and prove herself worthy of being more than a glorified bookkeeper.

What she found when she opened the back door of the bar-of-the-night was so much more than she bargained for. A mutilated body that bore an eerie resemblance to her ex, and a stint in handcuffs.

Maybe becoming a private investigator wasn't in the cards. Even with the guidance of her boss, Mike Edwards, and the other investigators of the Edwards Agency, Annie struggled to close a case. Add in her run-ins with the local cops, and things got messy.

Then bullets started flying. What really had her worried was that the second one wouldn't miss.

Edwards Investigations
The Rimer File

Copyright © 2024
by P.J. MacLayne

Edwards Investigations: The Rimer File is a work of fiction. All names, characters, events and places found in this book are either from the author's imagination or used fictitiously. Any similarity to persons live or dead, actual events, locations, or organizations is entirely coincidental and not intended by the author.

ISBN: 978-1-7349587-4-4

Chapter One

The mellow voice of Hank Jr. disappeared as Annie McGregor closed the bar's door behind her. She took a breath outside Flats Lounge to clear the cigarette smoke from her lungs. The alley stunk as bad as she expected. Courtesy of Pittsburgh's remaining steel mills, the stench of rotten eggs mingled with the odor of stale alcohol and piss assaulted her. It wasn't enough to disguise the coppery odor reminiscent of the time her grandpa had butchered a cow during her summer visit to his farm.

Annie stepped out of the small circle of shuddering light from the fixture over the bar's back door to explore, fearing she'd regret it. She needed to stay focused on Bobby Hansen, but he was in the bathroom puking his guts out, so she could take a moment. The blood might be from a stray dog that had fled from a fight, but she doubted it.

A scrawny gray cat brushed her ankles. She jumped back. At least, she thought it was a cat. She didn't want to consider the other possibility. Her eyes roamed the alley, wondering how many other inhabitants of the passage she'd disturbed.

That's when she spotted him.

One arm lay outstretched on the

pavement, the other curled against his chest. The stained wife-beater shirt did nothing to hide the multiple seeping stab wounds. For the barest of moments, she thought the corpse was Ian, her ex.

"What are you doing in this part of town, Mrs. McGregor?" asked the plainclothes officer hovering over her, going through her purse.

She was seated on the curb, her legs stretched out, in front of the now-closed bar. She rolled her shoulders, trying to ease the strain caused by having her hands cuffed behind her back, then craned her neck to look up at him. He was as tall as a professional basketball player, so it made it that much harder to meet his eyes. "I'm working."

With the spare ammo cartridge from her purse in his hands, he stared at her.

"Not like that." Blood rushed to her cheeks and Annie hoped the darkness would cover her reaction. "I'm with the Edwards Agency."

"What's that? An escort firm? You don't fit the profile." His eyes raked her body.

She'd dressed down for the assignment. Torn jeans and a faded Johnny Cash t-shirt, her shoulder-length brown hair pulled into a messy ponytail. Was he making fun of her? She held back her anger. "I'm a private investigator, working undercover. You can find my business cards in my ankle holster. One of the uniformed officers confiscated it and my revolver." *After* she'd told him where she wore them.

"Diego," the officer shouted.

The cop who had shown up after the 911 call hurried over. They moved away, with their backs turned to her, and held a whispered conversation. Annie had no choice but to wait.

Annie considered the ramifications of her predicament. Had she blown her cover or added to her street cred? At least Hansen hadn't spotted her. He'd dashed out the front door, wiping his mouth with the back of his hand, as soon as the bartender had yelled that the cops were on their way.

The policeman in plainclothes—Annie had decided he was a detective, although he hadn't introduced himself—walked back and crouched beside her.

"When was the last time you fired your weapon?" he asked.

"Last Tuesday. Mike requires we practice on a weekly basis."

"Mike?"

"Edwards. Mike Edwards. My boss. He owns the agency."

"And cleaned it?"

"After practice, of course." Annie wasn't sure why it mattered. The dead guy hadn't been shot from the glimpse she'd had of the body.

"Let's get you out of those cuffs," he said. "You understand why we had to take precautions?"

"Of course, Detective..."

He grinned. "Myers. Detective Pierce Myers." He pulled a key from his dress pants pocket, turned her around, and unlocked the cuffs.

Annie groaned and brought her hands in front of her and rubbed her wrists. She stretched, stood, and stumbled.

Detective Myers was fast. He stood and grabbed her, steadying her. "You okay?"

"I stiffened up. Old injury." One that had nearly killed her a few years ago, when a van had run into her.

"How much did you have to drink?"

Pure cop, but Annie supposed it was his duty. "One rum and coke. And I suspect the bartender shorted me on the rum. I'm good, really. Just need to walk it out."

He let go of her, and she limped away. It only took a few steps until the knots in her left leg let go. The limp would never go away, but by the time she returned to where the detective stood, it was less pronounced.

"See?" she asked.

"You've convinced me. You've already given your statement to the responding officers, correct?"

"Yes." She remained calm, although she suspected she'd have nightmares of blood and knives once she went to bed.

He retrieved a business card from another pocket and handed it to her. "If you think of anything else, call me."

Annie thought she'd been thorough in the information she'd shared with Officer Diego, but perhaps some other detail might come to mind. She accepted the card and nodded. "I will."

Diego came out of the bar with Annie's gun and holster and handed them to Myers. The detective examined the gun and took one of the business cards. He pulled a small flashlight out of yet another pocket and shone it on the card.

"It looks real," Myers said.

It wasn't the only time that someone had accused her of being a fake, but it never got better. The first time she'd held one of her cards, and saw the name 'C.T. McGregor,' she felt such pride. She rolled her eyes. "Of course it's real."

"It's just unusual to run into a female PI, even in this day and age."

Annie hadn't planned for her life to go this way, but it was the 1980s and almost anything was possible. "No one else has, either. That gives me an advantage."

Diego chuckled. "She's got you there, Detective."

The scowl on Myers' face made Annie worry about Diego's future in the police department, but there wasn't anything she could do to help.

Myers thrust the holster towards her. "Go home, Mrs. McGregor, and stay out of trouble."

The early end to the night and the numerous nightmares meant Annie made it to the office early in the morning. As she waited for the coffeepot to do its magic, she pulled a blank copy of the daily report from a gray metal file cabinet in the center of the shared main room and took it to her desk. Mike was already in his corner office, but the door was closed, so she didn't stop in to say good morning.

Besides, she'd let Mike down last night, not getting any evidence in the investigation into Bobby Hansen. Bobby's wife was convinced he was cheating, but Annie had seen no evidence of it on her first night of following him. Mike had warned her not to expect too much, but she'd been hoping for a miracle. She was still trying to prove that he'd been right to take a chance on her.

Her report didn't have to be perfect; just a record of the events. Still, she'd make it as good as possible, so if the client wanted to read it, it would be legible and informative.

About the time she was ready to sign it,

Mike came and perched on the corner of her scarred wooden desk. "Good morning. I hear you had an interesting night."

How did he find out so quickly? "Who is your connection with the police department?" she asked, setting down her pen. He probably had several, since he'd spent a decade on the force.

He grinned. "I'll never tell. But really, how are you doing?"

With one finger, she traced the graffiti carved into the top of her desk. "I keep thinking that if I'd stepped outside a few minutes earlier, I could have saved his life. As it was, I didn't even check for a pulse."

"From the report I read, that was the right call."

"It doesn't feel like it. I let you down, too, by letting Hansen out of my sight."

"What? Were you hoping you'd catch him cheating on your first try? It almost never happens."

Annie had watched other investigators in the firm close cases in no time flat and longed to match their accomplishments. "Where do I go from here?"

"The budget the client gave me has room for several more attempts. My advice would be to wait. Based on my experience, Hansen will lay low for a few days, anyway." He took off his glasses and rubbed his eyes.

Which Annie noticed were bloodshot. "You're spending too much time trying to figure out the computer again, aren't you?" she asked.

"I thought I was a smart man," he said with a frown. "I should be able to use it, but it baffles me."

"Show me what you're trying to do." Annie pushed her chair away from the desk. "That's why you hired me."

As part of her rehab after her accident, she'd been offered a class in computer operating, and ended up taking several advanced courses as well. She wasn't an expert, but along with the typing classes she'd taken in high school, she'd impressed Mike at the interview for a backup receptionist.

Walking next to Mike always made Annie feel short. He was average height, but the way he carried himself made him seem taller than he was.

But the height difference was forgotten when she settled into his padded chair and stared at his computer screen. This was the one thing she could do better than anyone else in the agency. It was the perfect combination between her accounting degree and the computer courses. She paid no attention to Mike standing behind her and began typing. When he left, she didn't even look away from the paperwork.

Betty Cook, Mike's long-time secretary, brought her a cup of coffee.

"I've told you before, you don't have to do that," Annie said, rubbing her eyes.

"I wanted an excuse to warn you-you have a visitor from the police department. He's in the conference room and Mike is finding out what he wants. Standard procedure."

"Let me guess-Detective Myers." Annie was glad she'd worn her black business suit. It might make the detective take her more seriously.

"You got it in one. Mike will sit in on the interview if you want."

She knew enough about cops to want a witness. Her brother had taught her many of their tactics. Annie ran her fingers through her hair like a comb and prepared for the encounter.

The detective arched an eyebrow when she breezed into the meeting room, a full cup of coffee in one hand and a stack of paperwork in the other. Mike grinned and nodded.

"Good morning, Detective," she said as she settled into the chair on the other side of the table, the one that had the most padding. "How can I help you?"

"I'm following up on last night's incident, Mrs. McGregor. Have you remembered any additional information that might assist in the investigation?"

She took a sip of her coffee. *Answer the question, and nothing more.* "I haven't seen your report, so I don't know what your officers passed along. Is there anything specific you were hoping to follow up on?"

Myers cocked his head. "Did you see anyone else in the alley?"

That was one she could answer. "No. But people were in and out of the back door throughout the night."

"Is that normal?"

Trick question. "I don't know. I'd never been there before."

He sat silent. Annie guessed he hoped that she'd keep talking. She didn't. She used the moment to study him in the harsh artificial light. Dark brown hair in a military-style crew cut that almost hid the silver steaks. His suit looked more expensive than a detective should be able to afford. Enough lines in his forehead to show he was no rookie.

"And you were there because…?" he asked.

"I was on assignment."

"Which was?"

"Privileged client info." She glanced at Mike.

Mike, who was standing in the corner staying out of the way, jerked his chin to indicate his approval.

"We may need that information, Mrs. McGregor." The detective drummed his fingers on the tabletop.

"You'll need a warrant for that." Annie sat

back and waited to see if the detective would share anything more. She could out-wait almost anyone, thanks to lessons from her brother.

"Did you notice any unusual activity?" Myers asked.

It depends upon his description of unusual. "In what way? Can you be more specific?" Annie took another sip of her coffee.

"Don't play innocent. Drugs are an epidemic, and Pittsburgh isn't immune."

She had limited personal experience with the use of illegal substances, but was aware of law enforcement's ever-present concern with their use. She leaned forward. "Last night's crowd didn't seem to be the right bunch, Detective. I didn't spot anyone using drugs, and I wasn't offered any. The customers seemed more concerned with getting drunk."

Myers grimaced. "Our informant reported the same thing."

Annie almost felt sympathetic, but she couldn't allow her emotions to cloud her responses. She waited; the next step was his.

"Did you recognize the victim, Mrs. McGregor?"

"As I told the responding officers, I didn't see his face." She didn't know whether that was good or bad. It made it easier to disconnect from the body and the pain, but harder to mourn him as a person.

"Look at this and see if he looks familiar."

The detective slid a Polaroid across the table.

It was a bad photo. Whoever had taken the picture had jiggled the camera when they pressed the button, and the flash had been too close. The resulting glare obliterated the fine features. Annie suspected it hadn't been given enough time to process before the developing film had been ripped away.

She took her time studying the photo, trying to match it to any of the faces she'd seen at the bar. But her attention had been focused on Hansen, and the victim hadn't interacted with him. She took a second look, then shook her head.

"Sorry, I don't recognize him. There's nothing about his face that stands out. He's pretty generic looking. Short brown hair, no scars, no sign he wore glasses...do you have a name?"

"No wallet, so no. It appears to be a robbery gone bad. And no one has reported him missing, either."

"Fingerprints?" Mike left his corner and sat beside Annie. She handed him the photo.

"It'll take a few days to get the results," Detective Myers explained.

Mike took a moment to look at the shot. "Any chance I can get a better picture? I'd like to assist the department and see if my staff have run into this guy. I don't think this one will photocopy well enough to be useful."

"How big is your staff, Mr. Edwards?" Myers looked out the conference room's windows to the open office area with a few scattered desks in it.

"We're a small agency, but we have working relationships with others in town." He placed the picture on the table within the detective's reach. "It seems to me you need all the help you can get."

"You should leave police work to the professionals, Mr. Edwards. Stick to chasing down cheaters and stay out of trouble." The detective picked up the picture and stood. "That includes you, Mrs. McGregor. Thank you for your time."

It would have been polite to accompany the detective to the front door. Annie didn't.

Chapter Two

Another night, another bar.

Annie waited a week before borrowing Mike's old beige sedan and following Bobby Hansen to the Dazy, a hole-in-the-wall nightclub on the south side. Her backpack of assorted clothing held the wardrobe she needed to mingle with the other female patrons—a long-sleeved, neon pink shirt to go with a too-tight pair of jeans.

The one thing she couldn't fix was being older than everyone else. The customers seemed to be of college age. Hansen stuck out worse than she did. A lot of the girls avoided him, despite the multiple drinks he bought. This seemed to be a more likely spot for drug use, and she wondered if Myers had an undercover agent among the customers.

The multi-colored flashing lights mixed with the booming bass music gave Annie a headache. Or was it the hint of pot mixed in with the cigarette smoke? She wasn't sure how long she'd be able to stick around, but took comfort in knowing Hansen wasn't enjoying himself, either. Everyone but the bartender ignored him, and even the bartender avoided him as much as possible.

"You want another one?" the bartender

asked Annie. She'd taken a seat at the bar to catch her breath after dancing with a group of girls. They'd been trying to teach her the latest dance moves.

What she really wanted was an iced tea, but she didn't think that would be available. "How about a diet cola?"

"Quitting so soon?"

"Not my crowd. I suspect my coworkers told me to come here as a practical joke."

He grinned. "Not mine either, but it pays well."

It had been a long time since Annie had engaged in serious flirting. Or not-so-serious flirting. She smiled back. "Good tips? I'm surprised."

"It's easy when they're spending mommy and daddy's money." He turned away to get her a pop.

Annie used the moment to locate Hansen and found him huddled in a corner with a group of other men. There was a swift handshake that may have served as a cover for something more. Maybe it was an introduction.

"Here 'ya go," the bartender said. He put a napkin down on the bar and set the glass on top. "On the house. I'm Ron."

Annie raised the glass in a salute. "Thanks, Ron."

He left to serve other customers, and she toyed with the idea of sticking around in case he came back to chat. But she was working. Hansen wasn't having any luck picking up a companion, so there wasn't a reason for her to stay.

Annie shook two aspirin out of the oversized bottle Mike kept in his desk. Last night's headache lingered. "What if Hansen isn't cheating?"

"I've seen Mrs. Hansen's bank reports. Money is going somewhere. He's pulling cash from MACs, and she doesn't know what he's doing with it." Mike poured her a cup of water from the jug he kept by his desk. "It started off with the occasional $20 here and $20 there, so she didn't pay attention, but the amounts and frequency are increasing."

Mike was the only person in the company with his own office. It was sparsely furnished, with a scarred wooden desk, one bookshelf filled with outdated law books, and three metal file cabinets. He didn't have the money to create more offices in the old warehouse space. What the space did offer, besides the lack of nosy neighbors, was a basement he'd had converted into a shooting range.

"I didn't see any sign of him overspending," Annie noted. "No buying drinks for the house, no flashing cash. I'm going through the phone bills for the last few months, but not spotting anything."

"How about gambling?" Mike asked.

"I'm not an expert, but there didn't seem to be anything like that."

"I'll send you out with Rodriguez to a sports bar some time. He'll teach you a few things."

A tingle of excitement spiraled down Annie's spine. Alex Rodriquez was Mike's most experienced investigator and got the best assignments. "I'd like that."

"We'll wait until after you've completed the Hansen investigation. I want to keep you under wraps for now."

Sadly, it made sense.

Mike grinned. "Don't look so disappointed. You're my ace-in-the-hole. No one expects a female PI to follow them."

"You have more faith in me than I do."

"Give yourself time. How many changes have you been through in the past couple of years?"

Too many. The accident, the death, the divorce, the change in jobs. Annie gave herself a mental shake. "Don't say that to Detective Myers. He thinks I should be a housewife, or he'd be generous and let me be a secretary."

"The world is changing and Myers hasn't caught up." Mike shrugged. "You'll run into a lot of that. You can't allow it to affect the way you do your job."

"I checked the crowd for potential undercover cops last night."

"It's not a bad habit to get into. But don't believe the stories about being able to identify them by their shoes or their haircuts. The good ones don't fit the stereotypes."

"Were you a good one?" Annie knew little about Mike's background, but he'd been a policeman until he'd been injured on the job.

"Nope. I was a street cop. Proudly pulled on that uniform before every shift." He cocked his head. "And leave it at that, Annie. That's the first rule of working for me."

"I remember." Everyone had warned her to not dig into Mike's history, and she'd restrained her curiosity. So far.

If Annie spent too much time reviewing clients' phone records for the entire office, she'd need to get glasses. She leaned back in her chair and rubbed her eyes. Mike had warned her about this part of the job. It freed up the other employees to spend more time on their investigations. These records were part of a case Mike was handling. Once in a while, a friendly competitor, The Hillard Group, got overloaded and threw a case or two Mike's way, and he preferred to handle them personally. Except for the long list of phone calls made by the Nowak family.

Leon Nowak had supposedly torn the tendons in his left ankle when he'd tripped on the stairs at work and would require six or more weeks of time to heal. His employer didn't believe it and had filed a complaint. As a result, Mike was spending several hours a day watching Nowak's house and tracking his activities, a standard workman's compensation investigation. So far, no evidence of wrongdoing had been found. Which made digging through the phone records annoying but important.

And boring. Call after call to Nowak's mother. Occasionally a call to a friend. All on nights and weekends. Which was to be expected, since this was the bill before the accident happened and Leon and his wife both worked during the day. The bill for the month after should be more interesting.

Mike hadn't revealed how he got his hands on the records. She assumed he had a contact at the phone company, but the information was another of his well-guarded secrets. The paper was clean, so it was safe to believe he hadn't retrieved them from the Nowak's home's garbage. She'd heard the guys talking about those excursions, but she hadn't been on one yet.

As she worked on the Nowak's second

month's bill, the bell over the front door rang. Since she filled in for Betty, she glanced up to make sure that the older lady had it covered. Which she did, but it gave Annie time to mentally prepare for another encounter with Detective Myers, but without the steadying backup of Mike.

Betty had already provided Myers with coffee when Annie arrived at the conference room. "I'd ask you if you had an update on the murder, Detective," Annie said as she walked in carrying a notebook and pen, "but if you did, you wouldn't be here. Which means you want something from me."

"Good afternoon to you too, Mrs. McGregor." Detective Myers snapped.

Annie set the paper and pen on the table, walked out of the room, and closed the door behind her. She re-opened it and waltzed back in with a smile glued to her face. "Good afternoon, Detective. How are you? I hope your day has been going well. Please have a seat. How can I assist you?"

She stood, her hands resting on the back of a chair, and waited, trying to interpret his expressions. His lips narrowed, and he clicked his pen several times. Then he shook his head and chuckled.

"I asked for that, didn't I?"

It was a loaded question, and Annie didn't answer.

Myers scratched the back of his neck. "Out of curiosity, what department were you with?"

She cocked her head. "What makes you ask?"

"Putting two and two together. I know your boss is an ex-cop, so I figured you might be. But I haven't found anyone on the local force that knows you."

Not under her married name. There were a few cops that might remember the little girl that came to visit her big brother at the Centre Street office.

"I prefer it that way. Now, how can I help you, Detective?" She pulled out her chair and sat.

He pushed a manila file folder across the table. "We were able to identify the victim from fingerprints. Name is Harold Rimer. Turns out he has a long rap sheet. From there, we developed a list of potential suspects. Would you take a gander at these pictures and see if any of these people were at the bar that night."

She flipped through the folder to see if any one face stuck out before settling into a closer examination. "A motley crew," she said. "Lots of mugshots. Your victim must have run with an interesting crowd."

One picture grabbed her attention, and she pulled the photocopied sheet from the folder. "Is this a gotcha? That looks like Officer Diego." She pushed the photo back to Myers.

"That wasn't meant for you. I compiled these pictures to use in questioning his neighbors and the employees at the bar."

Annie gave him credit for a good cover story. She started at the top of the stack for a second, better look. Halfway through, she'd spotted nothing that would be helpful to the detective.

One faded black-and-white picture made her stop. She traced the lines of the face with one finger, then set it aside.

"You know who that is?" Myers asked.

"He reminds me of my Uncle Leroy. Same nose, same cheekbones. But my uncle died five years ago, and didn't have any sons."

"I'm sorry," he said.

"Thanks." He'd been her favorite uncle, but his death from cancer had been expected. Annie continued flipping through the pictures.

She stopped at another shot and crunched her eyebrows. "That's Ron."

Myers leaned forward. "Ron?"

"I don't have a last name for him. He was the bartender at a nightclub I was at last night. The Dazy. D-A-Z-Y."

"I'm not familiar with it." The detective shook his head.

"I doubt it's your kind of place. Wouldn't be mine, either, under other circumstances."

Myers chin jerked. "I told you to leave police work to us."

"But here you are."

"What can you tell me about Ron?" he asked, ignoring her remark.

"He seemed like a nice guy, but not like he belonged there. He said he was there for the money. And I didn't spot anything illegal going on, although the place gave off psychedelic vibes."

Myers scribbled in the small notebook he'd pulled from a pocket. "Do you have the address?"

"I didn't get it, but it's in an alley on the 500 block of Hill."

"We can track it down from that. Recognize anyone else?"

Annie returned her attention to the shrinking stack of papers. She'd always been one to pay attention to detail, so she took her time. At the second-to-last sheet, she stopped again and studied that face. Something about the eyes bugged her.

"Is he another one of your ringers?" she asked, turning the picture so Myers could see it.

He read the information at the bottom. "No. You recognize him?"

"I'm usually good with faces, even if I don't remember names. I think I should know this one, but I can't place it. Maybe I've run into him in the grocery store or something."

"Not at the bar last week?" Myers asked.

"No. It's an older memory than that. What's his name?"

"Charlie Daniels. Obviously fake, but the arresting officer wasn't a country music fan."

Annie chuckled. "Or some poor soul with bad luck when it comes to his name." She closed the folder. "Sorry I couldn't be of more help, Detective."

"One lead is better than none." He pushed his chair back and stood. "I appreciate your help."

"Before you go, can you tell me something? Did Harold Rimer have a family? Have they been notified?"

Myers stopped by the door. "He was not a family man, Mrs. McGregor. He had one son who is a guest at a federal penitentiary. For murder. The report I received is that his son's reaction was something similar to 'Good riddance.' Cleaned up, of course."

Chapter Three

Annie pulled on the cowboy boots she hadn't worn since high school. They were half a size too small, and she'd regret it in the morning, but they were perfect for the job. "What does this have to do with being a PI?" she asked.

From across the desk in his office, Mike checked the clip of his revolver and chuckled.. "Nothing. I'm doing this as a favor for a friend. Coulson Nation offers bodyguard services through his agency, but he doesn't have enough manpower tonight."

"Doesn't the Civic Center have their own security staff?" Annie tugged to adjust the pink-checkered flannel shirt she'd pulled from the back of her closet. A few stubborn wrinkles remained but they helped disguise the shoulder harness Mike had lent her.

"Yes, but this guy's contract specifies armed guards. A few years ago, he had an issue with an aggressive stalker. Word is, the culprit is back on the streets. Most of the arena's staff aren't gun- trained and the cops they usually contract with are tied up with a Pirate's game."

"So we're second string?" Annie asked.

"More like third." Mike tucked his revolver into his waistband at the small of his back. "But it's a break from following cheating spouses. And it'll be a good experience for you."

"What exactly will I be doing?"

"Hanging out with the backup singers, mostly. Sorry for the typecasting, but Coulson jumped at the opportunity to have personnel in the women's dressing room instead of outside in the hall."

She raised an eyebrow. "You're being awfully cagey about the details of this assignment. You still haven't told me who the celebrity is."

"Standard procedure. That way, we can't tell anyone ahead of time. I know who it is, of course, but I won't get the official word until we get there."

"But you know," she insisted, feeling insecure and left out.

His grin stretched across his face. "I called the box office and listened to the list of upcoming concerts. Basic investigative work."

Annie would have thought of that.

Mike pulled a cowboy hat from the bottom drawer of a file cabinet and slapped it on. "I'll tell you on the way. Let's ride."

The hills and narrow streets of Pittsburgh challenged even the best of drivers, but Mike negotiated them like a rally car driver. It made

Annie even more insecure. She'd never match his skill.

"He's an old country western singer," Mike said as the engine idled at a red light. "I don't listen to that kind of music, but he was popular enough in his prime that his name rings a bell."

Annie suspected he was teasing her by not telling her the singer's name. Or was it a test? She stared out the car window, pretending to study the flow of pedestrians crossing the street. "He can still sell enough tickets to fill the arena?"

The light turned green and Mike didn't answer. He concentrated on joining the flow of traffic on the cross street. "I don't know," he answered once he'd made it to the right lane of traffic. "But the smaller the crowd, the easier our job will be."

"You still haven't explained what our job is," she said.

"Yours is to make sure no one gets too enthusiastic in their admiration for the ladies— the backup singers. Don't let anyone who doesn't belong in the dressing room. Scowl as you walk with the ladies to and from the stage. Keep your eye out for anything out of place and anyone who doesn't look like they belong. Mostly, you'll be backup to arena staff."

"You make it sound easy."

"The hardest part will be convincing the staff that you're more than a pretty face."

Annie blinked. She didn't know how to take the statement. Was Mike trying to give her a compliment, or was it only a warning about how others might view her? Mike had always been strictly professional when dealing with her. Impassive was the word she used to describe him. "You make it sound easy, but I'm nervous."

"Coulson promised he'd pair you with one of his guys, Frank Axon. Standard procedure with new people. Frank will guard the dressing room from the hallway."

That helped. "You still haven't told me who's performing."

Mike kept his eyes on the traffic. "Russell. Dan Russell. Have you ever heard of him?"

Back in high school, posters of him had covered her bedroom walls. They'd played one of his songs for the first dance at her wedding. But she'd stopped following him when adult life took precedence. It hadn't been worth the fights with Ian, her ex.

"I've heard of him," she answered. "Way back. I thought he died."

"Nope. And it's our job to make sure he stays alive."

Annie had only been to the Arena one time with Ian for a Pittsburgh Penguins game, but hockey wasn't her sport and she'd never gone to another. Of course, they'd been in the cheap seats, and she hadn't seen the dressing room area.

Which is all she'd be seeing while on the job, according to Frank, her partner for the night. She might get a glimpse at the stage, but that was all. She'd never dreamed of being in the limelight, so she was okay with it.

Annie had never considered herself a small woman, but standing next to Frank made her feel like a middle-schooler. His presence was calming, even if she had to rush to keep up with him as they walked down the corridor.

"Take a good look at your nametag," Frank said. "It'll give you access almost anywhere. I've seen fakes floating around, so be careful. Memorize the placement of your picture and the colors, as well as the words. You'll be in the dressing room tonight, and I'll clear everyone who wants in, but you should check them, anyway. Good practice if you ever work with us again."

"How long have you worked for Mr. Nation?"

"I've been with him since he started the agency. We served in the Army together. Why? Are you thinking about applying for a spot?"

She shook her head. "Not a chance. I appreciate everything Mike has done for me in the short time I've been with him."

"He's a good guy. He'll take care of you."

One test down and passed with flying colors. How many more would Frank throw at her?

He stopped in front of an unmarked metal door. A solitary chair sat propped again the wall beside it. "This is our station. When the ladies are on stage, we'll hang out here to make sure no one sneaks in to surprise them when they come back."

"Do people really do that?"

"Over-eager fans go farther. I dealt with one that crawled into the costume trunk, hoping to get pictures of the ladies changing clothes."

"That's creepy."

"The chick stalking Russell is worse. She's followed him all over the country, camped out on his doorstep, faked being a pizza delivery driver and tracked what room he was staying in at a hotel, and more. He's got a reason to be paranoid."

"You'd think he'd hire his own bodyguard." Annie leaned against the wall, trying to ease the pressure of the too-small boots. With her back, she could feel the vibrations of the drums that were part of the sound check.

"Rich folks. I gave up trying to figure them out." Frank's walkie-talkie beeped, and he walked a few steps away.

Annie sat and wiggled her toes. She hoped there'd be a chair for her in the dressing room.

Frank was back in a few minutes. "The talent is on the way. Let's get to work."

Annie hoped that someone thought her presence was worth the money, because it seemed to be a waste of time. With Miranda, Kelly, and Tonya, the backup singers, on stage, there was no one for her to guard. She sat in the locked dressing room and wished she had a book to read.

Frank was either on the other side of the door or off taking care of business somewhere else. She couldn't be sure because they weren't allowed to use the walkie-talkies during the concert, and her orders had been to stay in the room. There was nothing in the room to entertain her. She had little interest in the vast assortment of makeup containers and other beauty aids scattered across the built-in shelf that served as a dressing table. The ease with which the trio had applied their fake eyelashes had amazed Annie-she'd never got the hang of it.

A single knock, a pause, another single knock, another pause, then two knocks was Frank's prearranged signal. It seemed silly, but Annie hadn't allowed her expression to change when Frank told her about it. He was the expert, and they were playing by his rules.

With her right hand, she reached into her shirt and unstrapped her gun, then cracked the door open and peeked outside. Yes, it was Frank, and he was alone. She relaxed and opened the door the rest of the way.

"Everything good?" she asked.

"Yep. We got the word that they'll be wrapping up in five minutes." Frank chuckled. "But depending on how many encores they do and how the audience reacts, that could mean thirty minutes. It's a full house."

"Then we'll be done for the night?"

"Nope. There'll be a meet n' greet in the club. That's when your outfit will come into play. You'll mingle with the crowd and watch for people who are acting suspiciously. If you spot anything, notify one of us and we'll follow up. You can tuck your nametag into your shirt."

That sounded like going undercover at a bar, which Annie was comfortable with. "Right. How many other of the guys will do the same thing?"

"Two or three. We keep our assignments flexible." He grinned. "I won't be one of them. I stand out like a sore thumb."

She grinned back. "At least you'll be easy to find if I need you."

Annie didn't like this setup. Too much noise, too many camera flashes, and too many people in not enough space. Clusters of fans stood by the large windows of the skybox, watching the band's equipment being packed up and chatting with each other. Other people gathered around the performers. Miranda, Kelly, and Tonya had drifted to different parts of the club, and Annie couldn't keep an eye on all three of them at the same time.

The biggest group of people gathered around Dan Russell, of course. Mike was one of several men guarding him, so Annie wasn't worried about him. She wished she could get his autograph, but that would be unprofessional.

Frank was gatekeeping the entrance. Every so often, she'd wander by him, nod, and continue on her way.

She tracked a stubby brown-haired guy who kept circling around Kelly taking pictures, but never tried to engage her in conversation. Annie couldn't decide if he was shy or had another motive. He hadn't done anything worth mentioning to Frank or another member of the team. But she wouldn't ignore him like she ignored the handshake and exchange of money for a tiny baggie of white powder. The illegal activity was none of her business.

Kelly, a tall brunette, strode over to the bar to get a fresh drink. Like Annie, she stuck to plain soda. Annie wiggled her way through the crowd to stay close enough to handle any overenthusiastic fans. From the corner of her eye, she watched as the short man she was worried about followed Kelly from a different angle.

She needed backup. She reached up and tugged on her left ear in the prearranged signal to the team for assistance. Mike hustled to her side.

He leaned down. "What's up?"

"Three o'clock," she said. "Short guy in a black shirt, with blue applique on the shoulders. He's been orbiting around Kelly all night. The creep factor is rising and I don't like it."

"Does he have the proper credentials?"

"I haven't gotten close enough to check."

Mike nodded. "I'll take care of it."

At the bar, Kelly chatted with a couple of fans. The bartender hung close by. Annie wondered if he worked for Coulson Nation on the side. She hoped so.

The lowlife moved into a space left empty by a trio of gray-haired women who giggled about staying up past their bedtime as they headed for the door. Too close to Kelly for Annie's comfort when she was unsure of his intentions.

She dropped her almost-empty red solo cup in a nearby garbage can and returned to the bar, pushing her way between the creep and Kelly. Annie nodded to the bartender, and he poured her another cola. He set it in front of her and tilted his head towards the questionable man. So, he was aware of the potential issue. She bobbed her head.

Emboldened, Annie turned, blank-faced, to face the chunky man. A risky maneuver, intended to force him into a fight-or-flight response. In the best scenario, he'd choose flight.

Chapter Four

Raucous laughter broke out from a group of partygoers near the wall of windows in the club room, but Annie never took her eyes from the creep's face. His pupils were dilated, and his hand shook as he rubbed his nose. Drugs. There'd be no guessing what he might do.

She was no saint. After the divorce, Annie had done her share of partying. Pot, mostly, but she'd sampled coke, too. They didn't mix well with the meds she'd been prescribed after the accident, and she'd never used again.

A quick squeeze of her left arm against her side reassured her that her weapon remained in place. Would she be fast enough to get to it?

He took a step backwards, but Annie didn't let her guard down.

"Get out of my way, bitch," he snarled, raising his hand to clutch a strap around his neck.

It wasn't just one strap, Annie realized. He had three cameras dangling against his chest. Not a normal fan, then. "What's your deal?" she demanded.

He stiffened. "If you make me miss the best shot of the evening, you'll regret it."

Russell had an assigned photographer,

and this guy wasn't him. Annie had met the official shutter bug when he came into the ladies' dressing room before the concert. At the moment, he was on the other side of the room, talking to fans.

If the creep was paparazzi, wouldn't he be taking pictures of all the artists, Annie wondered.

Not wanting to destroy the party atmosphere, she leaned in close and deepened her voice. "You and me need to have a little chat out in the hall." Annie placed her hand on his forearm and gripped it.

His eyes narrowed, and he pulled away. But Mike moved in on the other side.

"I'd do what the lady asks," Mike suggested.

The man's eyes shifted between Annie and Mike. Mike reached into his pocket and flashed his security badge. The creep nodded, and headed for the doors.

He didn't stop when he got to the hallway. Mike must have anticipated the move, because he gripped the man's shoulder and brought his flight to a sudden halt.

"Where do you think you're going?" Mike asked.

"You've got no right to keep me here," the man said, shaking himself free.

True. Annie had been told that all they could do was kick someone out unless they were caught in the middle of a crime. Even then, they had to wait for the cops to show up to handle the arrest. But how would this low-life know that?

"Who are the police going to believe if we tell them you were threatening a member of Mr. Russell's group?" Mike tapped the cameras hanging from the guy's neck. "I'd like to see what is on these."

The creep clutched the camera straps. "Look, can we talk? Somewhere where no one else will hear?"

Mike jerked his head down the hall. "Follow me."

They ended up in one of the skyboxes. Mike and the man took seats, while Annie stood by the hallway to keep them from being interrupted.

"Look, I'm just doing my job," the man said. "My name is Bouchard. Peter Bouchard. I'm a PI and I've been hired to get proof that Kelly Gatti is a cheater."

Mike's shoulders' tensed. "I've heard of you. You're from Chicago, right? You give PIs a bad name with the bogus situations you set up. How many people's lives have you ruined for the fun of it?"

"And who are you really working for?" Annie asked, moving away from the door to stand in front of Bouchard. "It isn't Kelly's husband."

"How would you know, girly?" Bouchard

sneered. "Low-rent eye candy like you needs to leave the real work to us men."

"Back off," Mike started, but Annie interrupted him.

"No worries, Mr. Edwards," she said, her voice honey-smooth. "I've been insulted by better. Let me handle this. Bouchard is the kind of man who is so scared of women that he has to put them down to make himself feel better."

"Everything okay in here?" Coulson Nation strode into the skybox, He wasn't a big man, and with short brown hair and brown eyes, he wouldn't stand out, but he brought with him so much energy that it made up for what he lacked in height. The deep crease in his forehead made it clear he wasn't happy. "Who do we have here?"

Annie suspected Coulson already knew, but it was all part of the game.

Mike answered. "You've heard of Peter Bouchard, right? He decided to bring his particular flavor of slime to our doorstep."

The crease in Coulson's forehead was joined by more wrinkles. "On what business?"

"None of yours," Bouchard snapped.

"He claims he's trying to catch one of the backup singers cheating," Annie said. "Which I know is a lie. Perhaps he has a client, but it's not the husband. More likely he's working for Russell's stalker and is using Kelly as a cover story."

A ghost of a smile crossed Coulson's face. "Is that true, Bouchard? Because there's a restraining order in place that makes you an accessory to a crime. I can call in a favor and get our local cops involved."

Bouchard's face reddened and he abruptly stood. "We're done here."

"Not until we say so," Mike said as he rose and joined Annie in blocking Bouchard's path. "When we think it's safe."

"I can take care of myself."

"Maybe." Annie smirked. "But there's a few of the roadies that could give you a run for your money. And if they teamed up. . ." She shook her head.

"You talk tough for a little girl that needs two-not one, but two-men to back her up."

I'm a lot tougher than I look and have the scars to prove it. But that wasn't information Annie would share in present company. "At least I have friends."

"For your protection, we'll provide an escort for you to your car," Coulson said. "And to make sure you leave. If you come back, you'll be busted for trespassing. I'll lay odds it won't be the first time."

Bouchard threw his hands in the air. "Whatever."

Annie didn't expect Bouchard to give up that easy. She didn't trust him. But the odds against him were overwhelming. Either that, or he'd gotten what he'd needed on one of those cameras.

She couldn't share her concern with Mike when Bouchard was in listening distance. And Coulson had stepped out in the hallway to talk on his walkie-talkie. Frustrated, she wondered if she could trip and knock him to the floor, damaging the equipment or ruining the film.

Frank, along with a member of the arena's security team, joined Coulson in the hallway. Annie approved. Bouchard had no chance of sneaking off with Frank as his watchdog.

Coulson beckoned to her to join them. Like a high-schooler summoned to the headmaster's office, she wondered if she'd done something wrong. She steeled herself before scooting around Bouchard and walking the short distance to the hallway. Frank gave her a single nod, which she interpreted as encouragement.

Coulson got right to the point. "What alerted you to Bouchard?"

"He didn't act like an average fan," she answered promptly. "Even though he'd dressed like one. He never approached anyone for an autograph or try to say hi. And he wasn't talking to anyone else. I was worried he planned to hurt Kelly."

"And that's why you signaled for back up."

"I'm happy I was wrong." Annie rotated her neck trying to ease the tension in her muscles. "But what is he really after? I'd sure like to see what's on those cameras. Is there any way you can confiscate them?"

Coulson grinned. "Legally, no." He and Frank exchanged a glance. "Legally."

They had something up their sleeves. Annie wouldn't ask what.

With Bouchard escorted from the premises, and Russell and his band on their way to their hotel, Coulson and his group gathered for a debriefing at a nearby 24-hour restaurant. The A-team of Mike, Coulson, and Frank sat in one booth, while Annie and Owen, another of Coulson's guys, sat three booths away. That gave Annie time to stretch out her legs and wiggle her feet. She wished she could take her boots off.

As Annie glanced through the menu, she tried to figure out how Owen fit in. A lanky mid-twenties man, his wardrobe of a faded black t-shirt and worn jeans made him perfect for undercover work, but his constant fidgeting drew too much attention. She hadn't noticed him at the concert, but was sure Coulson had included him for a reason.

After they'd ordered, Coulson left his booth and casually slid in next to Annie. "How'd you do?" he asked Owen.

Owen grinned. "Two out of three ain't bad." He reached into his pocket and slid two film containers over the table. "The third camera was a model I've never dealt with before and I didn't have a chance to figure out."

"You stole his cameras?" Annie asked.

"Nope. Just the film." Coulson chuckled. "Owen is my resident sleight-of-hand expert. He did an apprenticeship with a magician, but developed a condition that gives him the shakes. People believe he's on something and ignore him, and then when he bumps into them, are so busy yelling at him that they don't watch what he's up to."

"I have a day job," Owen explained. "I only do occasional favors for the Nation Agency. Coulson asked me to hang out in the parking lot tonight as a precaution."

"There's a reason you're telling me your secret," Annie said, not understanding Coulson's motive.

"I'm hatching a scheme, and the two of you are key. But I wanted your permissions before I take it further."

"Should Mike be included in this discussion?"

"It was partly his idea. But we don't want either of you to feel any pressure to agree."

"Exactly what are you talking about?" Owen asked.

"Trading off your skills. Like tonight. Mike

and I already do favors for each other, but we want to expand our informal setup to include the two of you." Coulson propped his elbows on the table and rested his chin on his clasped hands. "It wouldn't affect who your boss is."

Annie frowned. "You only want me because I'm a woman?"

"That doesn't hurt, but Mike has been telling me about your computer skills. That's where the future is, and I'm upset that Mike got the jump on me."

"That's not all I do. Mike is aware I don't want to spend my entire day stuck at a desk."

Coulson nodded. "He made that clear. How do you feel about infiltrating an all-women's gym?"

The restaurant's parking lot was lit up by red and blue lights and flashing strobes when Annie exited from the restroom. Mike, Coulson and Frank were staring out the windows, tracking the action. Owen had left earlier with the excuse he had to be up early in the morning. Annie sat next to Mike and swiveled her head to see what was going on.

"Traffic stop?" she asked.

"That's what we thought until your favorite cop showed up." Mike pointed to a group of police huddled around an unmarked car. "I can't imagine Detective Myers being assigned to traffic."

"I'd suggest sneaking out a side door but he's parked right by your truck." Annie peered out the window, but the flashing lights made it impossible to distinguish any details.

"Is he a problem?" Coulson asked.

One side of her mouth rose. "If you asked him, he'd say I was the issue. I'm an amateur getting in the way of professionals."

"I heard the same thing when I started. It isn't you. A lot of cops feel that way." Coulson grinned. "I don't know if your boss was an exception."

Mike shook his head. "Nope, not going there. No matter how I answer, you'll find a way to twist my words."

Coulson leaned back. "Good call, but it makes me sad that you aren't as easy to pick on as you used to be."

Annie wondered how long Mike and Coulson had worked together. It seemed an unlikely partnership. Coulson was laid back and Mike was anything but. He struck her as almost formal in his politeness. Or was that just with her? She'd never studied his interactions with the other employees.

The strobe lights outside dimmed and vanished as they were turned off, to be replaced by simple headlights. Annie blinked to adjust her eyes, then watched as the police cars pulled out of the parking lot, the unmarked car Myers drove leaving last. Tension drained from her shoulders.

"Show's over." Mike said. "Let's get out of here."

"Sounds like a good idea." Coulson grabbed the bill and held up a hand when Mike opened his mouth to protest. "Call it a bonus for you stepping in at the last minute, and bringing Annie along."

He turned to her. "Do you need a ride home?"

Chapter Five

Coulson drove a bright red Firebird and Annie was tempted to accept his offer of a ride, but her mother had taught her to always leave a party with the same guy she'd come with. "Another time," she said, trying to come up with a logical reason to decline his offer without insulting him.

Mike jumped to her rescue. "Annie stored her purse in the safe in my office. I'm taking her back to retrieve it and her car."

"Another time then." Coulson stood and stretched.

The party was over, so Annie slid out of the booth. She'd have to ask Mike if she could come in late. Well, later. She needed at least six hours of sleep to function, and it was already two in the morning. Thinking about it made her yawn.

It was catching. Mike covered his mouth politely, but Frank didn't hide his.

"No fair," Frank grumbled. "Take her home, Mike, before we all turn into pumpkins."

"So, what's the story with Coulson?" Annie asked Mike the next afternoon as he hovered behind her as she fixed the accounting spreadsheet again.

"What do you mean?"Mike asked.

"This is embarrassing, but I haven't dated anyone since my divorce and I'm out of practice. Was he making a move on me?"

He patted her shoulder. "Coulson is an interesting guy. I love working with him, but I wouldn't let him date my daughter if I had one."

"So, he's not picky about his partners?" Her ego deflated. For a moment, she'd enjoyed the idea that she was still attractive, despite her scars. She swiveled to study Mike's face.

"He flirts with just about anyone. He's more selective about dating. But he hasn't met a woman yet who can compete with the business. And yes, he was making a move on you. That's why I jumped in. I apologize if I overstepped."

"No, I appreciate it. I wasn't sure of the protocol."

"It's not on paper, but it's simple. Don't get romantically involved with a client, or anyone connected to a client. Impartiality is the name of the game." He frowned. "I guess I should create a policy about dating. That will give you an easy-out with Coulson, too."

"That means I have to cancel the date with Detective Myers," Annie said as she turned back to the computer.

She heard Mike's sharp intake of air, then silence.

"That would be against the new rules," he said slowly, as if the words were being dragged out of him.

Annie chuckled as she resumed typing. "Gotcha. So, what's the story about that all-women's gym Coulson mentioned?"

He grabbed another chair and sat beside her. "His client, Mr. Pearson, believes his wife is cheating, but there's no proof. She spends more money than he can account for, and suspects she's getting it from a sugar daddy. Several of Coulson's men have shadowed her and come up empty. The only place the wife goes they can't is the combination workout/dance studio. Even the staff there are women, and he thinks the client is delusional. But Coulson built his reputation on being thorough, and you're his ticket to protect it."

"I've been to a gym—once. It was filled with sweaty, overweight old men and muscle-bound guys who spent more time looking in a mirror than most women." Annie grimaced. "Promise me it won't be like that? Only with women instead of men?"

"I'm going to need a new outfit," Annie said as she slipped into the cab of Coulson's pickup, the one he used for surveillance.

Coulson raised an eyebrow. "You look fine to me."

She was wearing one of her standard business suits. Black pants, a white blouse and black blazer. Which was fine for signing up for a trial membership, but not for actually exercising. "Were you paying attention to the ladies who left a few minutes ago?"

One side of his mouth rose. "Yes. Those were some interesting outfits."

She'd caught him ogling the woman in a hot pink leotard with black tights and bright yellow leg warmers who'd walked by.

"Right. And I own nothing like that."

"Got it." Coulson took his wallet out of his pocket and pulled out a few bills. He handed them to Annie. "Is this enough?"

Most of Annie's wardrobe came from second-hand stores, and she didn't know how much the assorted parts of the outfit would cost. "It's a good start."

Coulson placed his wallet on the dash and stared at the entrance to the gym, where more members were leaving. It was a simple fake brick front, with no windows. "I won't be able to wire you for sound."

"And I won't be able to sneak in a camera. That will limit my ability to provide evidence for your client. Although I'm not sure what I'm looking for right now. Even the staff are women."

"You know about the birds and the bees,

right? But you are aware that sometimes it's the birds and the birds or the bees and the bees?" Coulson said with a straight face.

Annie's cheeks flamed. "I hadn't thought about that."

"I didn't either in the beginning, but I learned fast. I'll get Frank to take you out to a few of the gay bars in town." Coulson started the engine and waited for traffic to clear so he could pull onto the street. "After all, a cheater is still a cheater and you should be prepared for anything."

Why hadn't Mike had this conversation with her? "That makes sense," she said.

"Do you think you'll have the clothes you need by tomorrow?"

Rush hour traffic was already in full swing. Annie wasn't sure she'd be able to get everything she needed that quickly. "Do you know what days Mrs. Pearson usually goes to the gym and when? Is she taking one or more of the classes they offer?"

"Good questions. Let me check in with the guys."

"Then can we plan for next week? That will give me more time." What Annie didn't say was that she needed to find clothes that would hide her scars. Luckily, many of the styles available would do the job. If she wore them to and from the gym she wouldn't have to change in the locker room where another patron might see them. Sadly, it meant she'd have to pass up the jetted tub.

"I'll pass the word to Mike when I get the information. Keep him in the loop. Let him feel that he's still in charge of you." Coulson grinned broadly as he pulled into the parking lot of Mike's agency. "I have to stay on his good side if I want to keep borrowing you."

Despite the grin, something about what he didn't say bothered Annie. She wondered if he and Mike were really on as good of terms as they portrayed. That was all she needed – for her budding career to be destroyed by a private war between the two men.

The shoes were the hardest part. She didn't own a pair of sneakers because she couldn't get them modified to hide her limp. The long sleeves of the leotard hid the scars from the accident on her left arm.

It had almost killed her. The panel wagon lost traction on an icy hill mid-January and slid through the intersection. Annie had seen it coming, but with the cars in front of her stopped at a red light, there was nowhere for her to go. She'd unfastened her seatbelt and slid to the passenger seat before the collision. The doctors said that had saved her life. During her recovery, there had been days when Annie wasn't sure that was a good thing.

But she didn't plan to keep a membership at the gym long term, so it didn't matter. Just a day or two, a quick in-and-out, long enough to decide if Mrs. Pearson was doing more at the gym than exercising. Annie hoped she wasn't.

She tucked Mrs. Pearson's picture into her glove box. The lady was a stereotypical middle-aged urban wife, with mid-length bleach-blond hair, teased and hair sprayed for extra height, bright red lipstick, too much blush and eye shadow, and impossibly skinny. Annie saw women like that every time she went grocery shopping, usually with two or three kids.

But the Pearsons' didn't have any children. Which would be a good thing if Mrs. Pearson was cheating.

Annie flashed her membership card at the receptionist.

The giggly teenager gleamed a broad smile. "Don't forget, if you want to take any of the dance lessons, there's an extra charge. We have a great Jazzercise session starting in fifteen minutes."

That sounded like doing calisthenics in high school gym class. "Not today. I need to stick to the basics until I'm in a little better shape. I have plans for the stair machine."

She could climb one of Pittsburgh's famous stairs, but the machines had a good view of most of the gym. Which wasn't much to look at. The walls were grimy; the equipment worn out, and the floors had bare spots. There were brightly colored posters on the walls, but they did little to cheer up the industrial atmosphere. Box and ceiling fans stirred the air, but did nothing to hide the odors that rose from perspiring bodies.

The scenery wasn't why Annie was there. According to the case notes, Mrs. Pearson normally arrived around 10:30 in the morning. That was in fifteen minutes, so Annie kept her eyes on the front door as she climbed stairs.

She'd worked up a sweat before her subject walked in. There was no missing her. The neon yellow leotard was too bright when paired with the shocking pink tights. The gleaming, sparkly purple headband with a huge lime green bow drew all eyes to her.

"She's too old to be playing disco queen," muttered the lady, dressed in an outfit in shades of gray, who was working out next to Annie.

Annie had lucked out, meeting someone who knew all the gossip without any effort. "Do you know who she is?" she asked.

"Penny Pearson. Fair warning-her and her clique take over the stationary bikes and hold bitch sessions. She may be forty-something, but she acts like a high-school popular mean girl."

"Thanks. I appreciate it." The information destroyed the plan for her time in the gym. "I'm more out of shape than I realized. I guess I'll go work on my arm muscles and give my legs a rest."

Annie turned off the machine and stepped down, her legs shaking. Perhaps she should keep the gym membership after the case was over. Her physical therapist had suggested it but Annie had never followed up.

Penny sat on a bike, barely rotating the pedals, loudly discussing a recent movie with her friends. It all seemed innocent. Perhaps Mr. Pearson's suspicions were misplaced. There'd been nothing to suggest that Penny was closer to any one of the women compared to the rest.

But she kept glancing toward the front door, as if she was expecting someone.

From one of the side rooms, the wail of a saxophone reached her ears. It must be time for the Jazzercise class. Penny and her friends hopped off the exercise bikes and headed that direction, Penny hanging to the rear. A pixie-type lady stood by the door, and she hugged each woman as they entered. But if Annie's imagination wasn't running wild, it was more than the average hug that Penny and the lady shared. And the air kisses meant nothing, right?

After Penny strolled into the room, the instructor held something up, then tucked it into her bra. Annie wouldn't solve the puzzle today. As a trial member, her time was limited, and she'd used it up for the day. She wiped down her machine, stuck her towel back in her bag, and pulled on her jacket. The case had been in process a long time. A few more days wouldn't be the breaking point.

A police car, its sirens wailing, screamed by on the street as Annie walked through the parking lot. At least she didn't have to worry about running into Detective Myers on this case.

Chapter Six

The guilty returning to the scene of the crime, Annie thought, as she surveyed the Flats Lounge after following Bobby Hansen here from his home. Penny Pearson might not be fooling around, but her gut told her Bobby was. He'd made a stop at a Chinese restaurant, but must have eaten his food on the way here. Annie had pulled a Pirates baseball cap out from behind her seat and tucked her hair under it. She wouldn't fool someone paying attention, but the men in the bar weren't checking her out.

He was chatting with a skinny blonde who didn't look old enough to be in the bar, but they didn't seem serious. They spent as much time yelling at the TV—the Pirates were losing—as they did talking. When they were joined by another man, Annie decided she'd wasted another night.

When the second man slipped his arm around the blonde, the move confirmed Annie's judgment. She sipped her beer and checked out the other customers, wondering if any of them was an undercover cop. No one stuck out.

The man with Bobby stood, drawing Annie's attention. Bobby offered his hand, and the quick handshake included a flash of green. She waited for a second exchange, for a little baggie with white powder or perhaps weed. But nothing.

That was weird. What was Bobby buying? Or was he a gambler? She'd have to talk to Mike about it, see if Bobby's spending matched the profile.

Bobby finished his beer, and Annie decided the excitement was over. No trip to the alley tonight, and hopefully no police detective waiting for her outside. She looked forward to her bed and a book.

"I think Annie's right," Jorge Weisback, another of Mike's employees who had shadowed Hansen several times, said the next afternoon. "Nothing else makes sense."

Mike tapped his pen on his desk. "If he's gambling, what is he spending his winnings on? His wife isn't seeing any extravagant purchases."

"Unless he never wins," Jorge smirked.

"Or he's playing for such low stakes that all his winnings do is cover his next bet." Mike tossed the pen onto his desk. "No offense to either of you, but I'm going to take a stab at following him."

"Random idea," Jorge said. "The two of you go. Like a date as a cover. Better yet, a couple having a fight. No one will suspect you're

PIs."

Mike and Annie exchanged a glance. "I don't know if I'm a good enough of an actor to carry that off." Annie brushed a speck of dust off Mike's desk. "The fighting part. I might be able to stage an argument with you, Jorge, but with my boss?"

Annie wasn't any good at fighting. She'd rather walk away than argue. During the divorce, Ian, her ex, had seen it as a weakness and exploited it every chance he had. She was getting better at it now that she was out from under his control.

"We'll make things work." Mike grinned. "Pretend I'm Detective Myers."

"You shouldn't have mentioned him," Annie groaned. "Now he'll show up."

Jorge chuckled. "Three times. You have to say the name three times for that to work."

"Is he still bugging you?" Mike asked. "The police closed the case. They don't want to spend any money trying to figure out who killed a low-life like Rimer. There are cops who believe that whoever did it performed a public service."

A vigilante? Still, could murder ever be justified? "Call me a bleeding heart, but it seems wrong to just throw Rimer away. What if his murder is tied to another crime?"

"That's where I get to say that you need to stay out of it. That's not what you're getting paid for. It's up to the police."

"Yeah, yeah. I know." Annie wished she had her brother to talk to. He'd understand.

Not knowing where Bobby Hansen was going made choosing an outfit a gamble. That's why Annie kept a box of clothes behind the seat of her truck. She didn't have the luxury tonight as they were taking Mike's beige car.

Throw in the added pressure of being on a not-a-date. Annie had chosen her wardrobe with care—decent jeans, a pale-blue t-shirt under a deep blue, silky blouse—she'd be able to blend in many places. To be on the safe side, she'd brought several additional t-shirts from her concert-going days.

Not for the first time, she checked to make sure the walkie-talkie was turned on. Jorge had the other one at his spot a block away from the Hansen's house, waiting for him to leave. Then Jorge would track him to wherever Bobby ended up for the evening. From there, Mike and Annie would take over.

"Nervous?" Mike asked. He'd reclined his seat and closed his eyes, appearing to be asleep.

"More like anticipation." Annie put the walkie-talkie on the dashboard. "I feel like I've let Mrs. Hansen down and this is my last chance to make it right."

Mike cracked an eye open and closed it again. "You're in the wrong job if you think you can fix every client's problems. Sometimes the information we uncover makes things worse. If you can't handle the reality of the job, you should look into a different field."

"Are you firing me?"

Both of Mike's eyes popped open, and he turned to study her. "Where did you get that idea?"

"What you said about finding a different job." Annie stared out the windshield.

"Don't be so paranoid. I tell everyone the same thing. Are you enjoying working for me?"

The walkie-talkie beeped. Annie grabbed it and pushed the button to talk. "Talk to us, Jorge."

"Hansen is heading east. That's new," Jorge reported. "I don't have a clue where he's going."

Mike started the car and nodded to Annie to push the button. "How is he dressed?"

"Khakis, a green polo shirt, looked like athletic shoes. Covers a lot of ground."

"Follow him and keep us informed. We're headed in your general direction." Mike pulled onto the street. "Any ideas, Annie?"

She'd spent over an hour reviewing the case files that afternoon. "No. Would Mrs. Hansen let us know if he had a work or social event? He usually doesn't dress that nicely."

"A birthday party?"

"Something like that. I guess we'll find out when we hear from Jorge."

Mike took a series of side streets that headed east. "It's problematic when a subject has an abrupt change in routine. All the work we've done means nothing."

"You've seen this happen before?" Annie asked.

"Once. I was contracted to follow a college student by her parents, who were worried she was getting pulled into heavy drug usage. Which she was. But she got scared, found religion, and straightened out her life. I didn't want to charge her folks anything, but they insisted, and I gave them an extremely discounted rate."

"How did you pull that one off?"

"I'm not a miracle worker, her friends did all the work." Mike pulled into a convenience store's parking lot. "I just dropped a few words in the right ears."

She cocked her head. "Have you dropped a few words to Hansen's friends? And how did you find them? The case files reported even Mrs. Hansen doesn't know who they are, other than a few from his college days."

A beep drew their attention. "He's stopped at a mom-and-pop video store," Jorge reported. "Next door to a pawnshop. Gee, I wonder where they get most of their tapes?"

Mike scrunched his mouth and took the walkie-talkie from Annie. "You think he's on to you?"

"That's all I can come up with. I drove down the block, but the way the strip mall is set up, I lost sight of him."

"Snag the address of the store and tomorrow you can go check it out. We're done for the night."

"Right. See you in the morning,"

Mike handed the walkie-talkie to Annie and backed out of the parking spot. "All dressed up and nowhere to go," he muttered.

Was he talking about her, Annie wondered. Or himself? "What do we do next?"

"I consult with Mrs. Hansen and see what she wants to do. It's her money."

Both Alex and Jorge had warned Annie that Mike didn't like to lose. Not just cases, but anything. On the ride back to the office, she kept her thoughts to herself.

"Raoul, my resident gadget guy, has figured out how you can take pictures of Mrs. Pearson," Coulson announced as he set a bright pink gym bag with black accents on Mike's desk the next day.

"That color won't draw any attention," Annie said sarcastically.

"But it matches that crazy outfit you wore last week," Coulson grinned. "And it looks like the ones everybody else carries."

Annie hadn't realized that Coulson had been spying on her. "How does it work?"

Mike unzipped the bag before Annie had a chance to grab it. "Interesting setup. What's the optimum range?"

"Twenty feet. Too close and the pictures are blurry." Coulson pointed to a round black spot on the side. "The camera lens is here, well hidden."

"Let me see," Annie said, hip-checking Coulson to move him out of the way. "I'm the one who has to use it."

Coulson laughed. "Right. Turn the camera on before you leave home. Hold the gym bag at whatever height you need and push this button." He pointed to a black spot near the zipper. "Raoul rigged it to connect to the shutter release. If you hold it down, it'll shoot a string of photos."

"How many pictures will it take?" Annie asked, peering at the small device strapped to the inside of the bag.

"Eight. That should be enough."

If she was in the right spot at the right time. "I'll find out this afternoon," Annie said, "when Penny shows up for the exercise group."

Annie timed her arrival for five minutes after Penny's normal workout time. She waved her temporary card at the receptionist and headed for the unused rowing machines. Penny and her crew were monopolizing the stationary bikes again. In their brightly colored athletic wear, they looked and sounded like a group of chattering tropical birds. Nothing worthy of a photo shoot, but Annie set down her gym bag with the camera lens facing towards the bikes.

She set the controls of her machine to the easiest setting, wanting to appear as if she was exercising without doing any hard work. But the rhythm of the bass bled from the dance room and Annie found herself rowing faster than she'd planned. She was almost disappointed when the booming stopped.

Penny and her friends gathered their belongings but didn't leave the bike area, even when the door to the dance room swung open. What were they waiting for? Then another lady joined the group, and Annie thought she spotted a flash of metal as she and Penny exchanged hugs.

She didn't have time to process the action before a new song started playing and the petite exercise instructor showed up in the doorway of the room. Penny and her friends waited for a few other women to shuffle into the room. Annie noted none of them got a hug. Then it was time for another performance of their ritual.

Annie waited for the door to the room to close before packing up, disappointed in the results of the surveillance. She'd failed Mike and Coulson once again.

At least the trip hadn't been a complete waste. She'd worked up a sweat, and she'd needed the exercise. A trip to the locker room would allow her to freshen up before heading home, even if she didn't take a shower.

A gray-haired lady glanced up when Annie entered, then went back to searching the oversize bag on the bench in front of her. "I know I put it in here," she muttered, unfolding and refolding a plain white t-shirt and setting it beside her bag,

As she washed her face, Annie used the clouded metal that passed as a mirror to watch the lady as she took one item at a time out of her bag and set them on the bench. Annie knew she shouldn't get involved, but couldn't help herself. "Is everything okay?" she asked, turning around.

The lady looked up, and Annie spotted tears on her cheeks. "My necklace," she said. "I put it in my bag, but it isn't there."

"Did it fall into your locker?"

"I used the inside pocket because of all the things going missing around here." Still, the older woman turned to the locker behind her and unlocked it using the key dangling from the elastic strap around her wrist.

Missing items? That changed everything. Curiosity bubbled, but Annie decided now wasn't the time to ask about it. Not when the lady was upset, and rightfully so. "Find it?"

She propped her right arm against the next locker and leaned against it. "No."

Annie heard sniffling. "Can you replace it?"

"My late husband gave the necklace to me."

Ouch. "Irreplaceable. Do you want me to check your bag? I'm Annie, by the way. I'm new. Thinking about joining." It was a no pressure way to get the other woman to introduce herself.

"Lucy. Would you please?"

Annie picked up the bag and shook it. Nothing rattled, but she hadn't expected it to because what appeared to be a set of car keys lay on the bench. She stuck her hand in the bag and felt around, but found nothing. The side pocket was next. Still nothing.

"What does the necklace look like, Lucy?" she asked.

"Nothing fancy, just a simple gold chain with a small opal pendant." Lucy sniffed. "My Joey got it for me on a whim and not for any special occasion."

"That doesn't make it any less important." Annie shook her head and checked for holes in the bag's liner. "I'm sorry, I don't see it. Did you leave it at home?"

"I put it on first thing in the morning.' Lucy put her hand to her lower neck, to the spot where a pendant would rest.

Annie had one more idea of where the necklace was, but she couldn't share it with Lucy. "Stop at the front desk and tell the receptionist. Someone might turn it in."

Chapter Seven

Annie drove her pickup to a nearby convenience store for a conversation with Mike. She flicked the switch on the walkie-talkie and waited for Mike's acknowledgment. "How much time can I put into the investigation?" she asked. "Coulson's report doesn't mention anything about Penny going to pawnshops."

"What are you hoping to find?" Mike's firm voice wasn't masked by the sound of papers rustling.

"It's too much of a coincidence. The missing items, Penny's clique, the way they interact with Honey, the trainer, the extra money that Penny's husband is worried about." She redirected the air conditioner to blow on her face.

"You think they are stealing from the other gym members?"

"Then pawning the goods and splitting the profits." Annie hesitated, hoping Mike wouldn't laugh. "It's far-fetched, but plausible."

"How do you plan to prove it?" he asked.

She tapped her short fingernails on the steering wheel before punching the transmit button on the walkie-talkie. At least he was taking her seriously. "I'll follow Honey. She's the next step."

"Hold off on that. Truth is, we should involve the police, but there's not enough evidence for a warrant. Besides, it would come out of Coulson's budget, not mine."

Annie eyed a blue van going down the street, but decided it wasn't Penny's and of no interest. "So, what's my next step?"

It took a long time for Mike to get back to her. "We'll talk when you get back to the office."

"Here's the thing." Mike placed his elbows on his desk and leaned forward. "Pawning jewelry doesn't bring as much money as people imagine. Certainly not enough to share with a group of people and be profitable."

Annie sat across from Mike while Coulson was on the speakerphone. "Well, that's another theory down the drain," Coulson's voice boomed over the phone. "Too bad, I liked it. You have any other ideas, Mike?"

"I'm trusting Annie's instincts and suspect something's going on, but I'm not sure it's any of our business." Mike's lips formed a tight line.

"If Penny is involved, it is our business," Annie insisted. "Besides, aren't you curious?"

"Misplaced curiosity will get you killed."

She'd learned that lesson when it ended

her brother's life. Official reports claimed differently, but Annie harbored unproven suspicions. There was no reason he should have been investigating the little Chinese restaurant down the block.

She forced herself back to the situation at hand. "Do you want me off the case?"

"Yes," said Mike.

"No," said Coulson. "I want to give the gym one more shot. Me and my guys have put too much effort to let it drop now."

Mike picked up a pen and clicked the end repeatedly. "What more do you think she's going to learn?"

"If I knew, I wouldn't need her to go back," Coulson snapped. "If it was one of your guys, you wouldn't question them continuing."

The pen pinged as Mike dropped it on his desk. He leaned back and studied the ceiling. Although Annie agreed with Coulson, she stayed quiet, not wanting to get involved in the argument.

"One more," Mike said. "With the stipulation that it is observation only. Annie is not to approach Mrs. Pearson or wear any jewelry that might tempt someone to steal it."

Had Mike read her mind? Annie ducked her head to cover the heat rising in her cheeks, pretending to glance through the case file paperwork. "I can live with that."

Annie glanced at her watch. Almost four. According to her research, Honey's last dance class had ended fifteen minutes ago, but Honey's pink compact car remained in the employee parking lot, a few spaces down from where Annie had parked.

Mike had stipulated that she couldn't contact Penny, but said nothing about Honey. A loophole, and Annie felt only slightly guilty exploiting it. Were the missing items at the gym a cover for something else?

Out of the corner of her eye, she spied a man dressed in dark clothing skulking a few cars back. She checked her doors were locked and her revolver was covered by her windbreaker on the passenger seat. It would be better if she never used it, but it gave her comfort that it was close by.

She checked Honey's car, which hadn't moved, and then her side view mirror. The figure was closer, and she recognized him. She put her gun under her seat, popped open the passenger door, and waited until he climbed in.

"Hey, Frank."

"What are you doing here?" he asked.

"Same as you, I suspect." She grinned. "Coulson send you? Or did you overhear the phone call and decide to do this on your own?"

"I've worked with the boss long enough to read his mind." Frank returned her smile.

Annie rolled her eyes. "You men are all the same. I'll never be able to prove that I'm competent if you keep trying to play white knights."

He shook his head. "Don't include me in that. I'm glad to mentor you, but I have no interest in holding your hand. I have enough to do."

"So, why are you here?"

"Because I'm curious. I want to see where this goes. Lord knows, we need fresh ideas."

His confidence in her was what she needed.

The back door of the gym opened and several of the employees walked out. They stood by the door and lit cigarettes. Honey was with them, but she didn't light up.

"That's her," Annie said, poking Frank in the shoulder. "The little one."

"She doesn't look like a common criminal."

"Nope. Perfect cover. You want to ride along and see where she goes?"

He fastened his seat belt. "Let's do this."

Honey chatted with her coworkers for a few minutes before going to her car. Annie started her truck but waited. Mike had taught her a few tricks for following people. None of them applied in this situation. She'd have to use her wits to not get caught.

"Are you familiar with this neighborhood?" Annie asked as Honey pulled onto the street. "I'd like to find a side street that goes the same direction that she takes."

"Sorry, no. My normal assignments don't take me to upscale neighborhoods like this."

He said it with a straight face, but Annie didn't believe him. The street had the look of having seen better days. Houses on the edge of needing painted, lawns needing mowed, storefronts with badly painted signs and neon lights with half the lights not working. She signaled for a right-hand turn wanting to appear as if she was lost. "You have a nice sense of sarcasm."

He chuckled. "I save it for the right circumstances. It gets me in trouble with the wrong people."

"I can see that." Honey stopped at an intersection waiting for the traffic to clear and Annie pulled into a parking spot. It was a risky maneuver because Annie might get hemmed in by other cars, but she was trying to convince Honey that her presence was a coincidence.

She glanced in her rear-view mirror and then checked it again.

"Something wrong?" Frank asked.

Annie shook her head. "For a second there, I thought I spotted one of Mike's cars. But there are a million old beige cars on the road, so it's probably just my guilty conscience imagining things."

"How many cars does he have?"

"I know about two. I suspect there is at least one more."

Frank twisted around to look behind them. "I don't see anyone."

Annie put the truck into drive as Honey finally turned right onto the cross street. She let two cars go past before pulling back onto the street and returning to the chase.

"Nicely done," Frank said. "Mike teach you?"

"He passed the duty on to Jorge, one of the guys."

"I've bumped into him a time or two. He seems to be okay, although not as good as Mike. Or me."

Annie bit back the snarky remark that rose to her lips as she swung into the left lane, mimicking Honey's path. "It looks like she's heading home. There's a residential area down that side street."

"And you know that how?" Frank asked.

"I came through here when I was apartment hunting." That was after the divorce and the accident. The apartment had seemed nice enough in the ad, but when she went to look at it, both elevators had been out of service. That had sent the red flags flying in Annie's head. She didn't want to drag her injured leg up five flights of stairs after a long day at work.

He nodded. "We should verify it's not a shortcut to another business area."

"Absolutely. I won't give up until she walks in the door of her place. Would have been easier to get my hands on the personnel files, but I didn't have time to check out the security system." Annie shrugged as she eased off the gas pedal to create a bigger gap between herself and Honey.

At the same moment, Honey pulled into one side of the driveway of a duplex. Annie kept driving.

"I'll snag that address for you," Frank said. "That way you won't have to make a second trip through the neighborhood."

"Thanks. I owe you." For more than getting the address. His presence had calmed her jitters.

"You may work for the competition, but you're an honorary member of our team." Frank patted her knee. "We've got your back."

"How long has it been since you've been bowling?" Jorge asked as he pulled into the parking lot of Star Bowling and Lounge with Annie acting as copilot. They had taken Jorge's old Gremlin. It looked ratty on the outside, but she knew he'd had modifications made to the engine.

"High school, probably," she grinned. "Back when I'd go with a group of girls and we'd hang around acting silly and hoping to attract the boys."

"And I was one of those boys." Jorge laughed. "Going away to college saved me from ending up in a bowling league."

"Is your subject a member of a league?"

"Blair? Ha! He's your typical couch potato, from what I can tell. The only exercise he gets is lifting his fork to his mouth. And with his supposed injury, he's had to limit that." Jorge pulled into a parking spot at the far end on the lot. "But I found a flyer in his garbage about a company event being held here."

"It seems unlikely that a man sporting a bad right arm would show up at a bowling alley." Annie had reviewed the case files, a rare insurance fraud issue that had landed on Mike's desk. Occasionally, The Wallis Firm, another agency in town, would pass along work to Mike when they had an overload. Blair claimed that his right arm was permanently injured in a bumper car crash at a local amusement park and had sued the company. They were fighting it, of course, but so far Jorge hadn't been able to catch Blair in any activities that proved he was faking it.

"Unless he just wants to have a drink or two with friends." Jorge reached behind the seat and grabbed a small camera. "Do you have room in your purse for this?"

"So that's why you asked me to bring a big purse. Typical man."

"Consider it part of our cover."

"Yeah, yeah." Annie popped open her door. "Do I have to let you win, too?"

It didn't look like Blair was going to show up. Hazards of the job. At least, they'd had fun playing a few games. Jorge won all of them. Now, it was nearly midnight, but they sat at a table in the bar area killing time, not willing to give up.

With all the people around, Annie and Jorge couldn't discuss work, so they talked about anything but. The Pirates, the newest weatherman on KDKA, which steel mill was rumored to close next, the other customers. Nothing to hint that they were anything but a couple out for a date night.

The crowd began to thin and Annie used her hand to cover a yawn. She wasn't used to staying up this late. Then Jorge nudged her with his foot, and she was fully awake again. He jerked his head towards the front door.

She knew better than to look. She leaned forward, laid her hand over Jorge's, and asked softly, "Sling?"

Jorge nodded and brought his face closer to hers, as if they were going to kiss.. "We'll see how long it lasts. Slide your purse to me."

Her purse was in her lap, but not for long. Under the table, she passed it to him. When it got back to her, it was lighter and he clutched a small black rectangle.

He winked and rose. "I'll be just a sec. Don't do anything I wouldn't."

Annie didn't have to ask what he was up to. They'd both made numerous trips to the restrooms and snack bar to cover their surveillance. As he moved across the lobby, it gave her an excuse to swivel and watch him. And look for Blair.

Blair wasn't hard to spot as a group of people stood clustered around him. Jorge worked his way around the edge of the bunch. From Annie's point of view, there was no indication that the sling on his arm was fake. He was holding his soda cup in his left hand and using a straw to drink from it. Another dead end?

Then someone handed Blair a rental pair of bowling shoes. Unless he was left-handed, that was a game-changer. Annie longed to abandon the table and worm her way towards the alley where Blair and three of his friends had taken seats. But Jorge was a sharp operator, and he tugged on his left ear in a prearranged signal.

From her seat, Annie spotted Blair removing the sling and passing a bowling ball between his hands. That would likely be enough to satisfy the insurance company, but she and Jorge weren't in a hurry. Having pictures of Blair delivering the ball would be definitive evidence.

But Jorge wasn't having any luck getting into a position where he could snap pictures unnoticed. Annie could help with that.

She unbuttoned the top buttons of her blouse and pulled her hair out of its ponytail before standing. She wouldn't be able to carry off acting drunk for more than a minute or two, but hoped it would be long enough. Her limp would help her carry it off.

Annie wobbled her way towards the snack bar, but abruptly changed her path and headed towards the now empty station next to the one occupied by Blair and his co-workers. She ran her hands over the balls in the ball return and picked up a pink one. She limped her way to the foul line and stood there, then turned around.

An alley employee headed her direction and Annie dropped the ball on a chair. From the corner of her eye, she caught several flashes. Satisfied her work was done, she brushed by the employee, grabbed her purse, and headed toward the front door.

Chapter Eight

"Jorge reports you were brilliant last night," Mike said.

To hide the reddening of her cheeks, Annie bent her head over the keyboard of Mike's computer. She was entering receipts and invoices to get Mike's books up to date. "I'm glad it worked out. With as much work as Jorge put into the case, I didn't want to lose the one chance he had to get his evidence."

"Quick thinking is an asset in this profession." Mike placed his hand on her shoulder. "You're coming along fine. It helps to make up for the trick you pulled the other night."

Shit, he knew about her and Frank following Honey. "It was an impulse."

Mike removed his hand and walked to the front of the desk. "Look at me, Annie."

She lifted her head and stared into his hazel eyes. The closeness made her uncomfortable, and she sat back in the chair.

He shook his head. "If you going to work here, you have to trust me, Annie. It's the same for everyone. We back up each other, and we can't do that without letting people know where we are and what we're doing."

Frank had been with her, but that didn't count, Annie assumed. "Who backs you up,

Mike?"

"I have my ways."

She didn't like it, but didn't push. He wouldn't tell her, anyway. "Message received. I'll finish these and get ready to follow Hansen tonight."

"No. I meant to tell you. Leona-Mrs. Hansen-called. She and Hansen will be out of town for a week. So, you'll have a week to concentrate on other things."

"Do you have another assignment in mind? Can I follow Honey again?"

"One question at a time." Mike laughed. "No on Honey. Yes on a new assignment."

Annie saw why Mike wanted another person in the conference room. Mrs. Ilene Stanwich could barely make it through a few sentences without breaking into tears. Annie made sure a box of tissues sat near the heavy-set lady's right elbow and her water glass remained full.

"It's been five years since I've seen my Kathleen," Mrs. Stanwich sobbed. "She and her father didn't get along, but I never expected her to leave the day she turned eighteen."

"Where did she go?" Mike asked,

"She planned to spend the afternoon at a friend's house, then we were going to take her out for a birthday supper. We had reservations at my husband's favorite steakhouse."

Mike and Annie exchanged a glance. Why not the daughter's favorite restaurant?

"Did something happen at supper?" Mike asked.

"She never returned," Mrs. Stanwich wailed. "At first, I thought she'd gone to her room to take a nap, but when we checked, she wasn't there. When we called her friend's mother, she told us Kathleen wasn't there."

"What did you do then?" Annie asked.

"After supper," Mrs. Stanwich started.

Mike interrupted. "After supper?"

"The reservation was hard to get." The lady sniffed. "Herbert didn't want to miss out. He figured Kathleen would show up when she got hungry. We had cake at home."

"Then what happened?" Annie asked.

"We got home around ten, but she still wasn't there." Mrs. Stanwich reached for another tissue and blew her nose. "That's when we realized her bedroom window was open and most of her clothes were gone."

"Anything else missing?" Mike asked.

"Nothing worth anything."

"Did she leave a note?" Annie asked. "And did you keep it?"

"Herbert ripped it up before I read it. But all it said was for us not to try to find her. And when he realized she'd stolen money, he forbade me to search for her." Mrs. Stanwich blew her nose. "He died two years ago."

Mike scribbled on his notepad, and Annie hoped he was writing the same questions bouncing around her brain. "So you haven't looked for your daughter for five years? Why now?" Annie asked.

Mrs. Stanwich broke into tears. Annie patted her on her back while shooting Mike a glance. Calming upset women wasn't her area of expertise. She hoped Mike was better at it.

"I just miss her so much," the lady said between sobs.

Mike poured a glass of water and set it in front of her, then waited until she had composed herself. "We'll need more information, and I won't make any promises, but we can try to find her. Our standard rates are on the paperwork I sent after our phone call. If you accept the contract, Ms. McGregor will be your primary contact."

"Is she any good?" Stanwich huffed.

With an arch of his eyebrows, Mike nodded. "If she wasn't, she wouldn't be working for me."

He said it, but did he mean it, Annie wondered.

"Here's the start of your new case file," Mike said, dumping a small stack of disorganized papers on Annie's desk.

"Mrs. Stanwich signed the contract?" Annie asked, reaching to the bookshelf behind her and grabbing several manila folders. From the way the corners of the papers pointed in every direction, her first task was to organize it.

"No, she wants her lawyer to check it. But she gave me a retainer that will pay for several hours of research."

"It won't be enough. Kathleen could be anywhere in the world. Or she could be dead."

Mike cocked his head. "What's your first impression?"

"That Kathleen had good reasons to leave home and was smart enough to wait until she was legally an adult to do it. She may have had help from a friend. Find that friend, and they might still be in touch with Kathleen or know where she is."

"Good start. What else?"

"While I'm checking Kathleen's death records, I want to check Mr. Stanwich's, too. I need to know when he died, and why Mrs. Stanwich took this long to decide to find Kathleen."

"That struck me, too." Mike pulled a chair from the empty desk next to Annie and sat. "She didn't directly answer most of my questions. She's hiding something."

"What restrictions do I have in the investigation?"

"None. But start with the straightforward stuff. You can gain Mrs. Stanwich's trust with some basic results, like hopefully no arrest or death records. At least not locally."

Which meant a lot of time spent poring over police records and microfiche. Annie suspected Mike was punishing her for her unauthorized expedition the other night. But he hadn't mentioned taking her off Penny's case. Or it was her guilty conscience working overtime.

"It's like changing personalities," Annie muttered, glancing at herself in the cloudy mirror in her bedroom. The bright clothes she wore for her trip to the gym made her appear like a different person than the one that had spent the morning in the public library glued to the microfiche machine. She hadn't found any information about Kathleen except for a listing about her high-school graduation, but her parents rated mentions in articles about a variety of fund-raisers.

She'd found Mr. Stanwich's obituary from two years ago, but not even a death notice for Kathleen. That was good. Something about the obit bothered Annie, and she printed it out to review later.

The whole day had felt off. Something wasn't right. What, she didn't know. But she'd asked Mike to swap cars for her trip to the gym. So, his little beige car was parked on the street in front of the apartment building.

She fluffed her hair and her courage before grabbing Mike's keys and heading out the door.

Road construction destroyed her timing, and Annie ended up behind Penny as they reached the gym's parking lot. To cover her tracks, she circled the block. Penny was already at the front door when Annie turned off the engine. Honey rose from a nearby bench and joined her.

So, those greetings before the classes were all an act. Annie should have figured that out. Was this a planning session for what to steal?

With her gym bag hoisted over her shoulder for easy access to the camera, she made her way towards the front desk to sign in. The girl at the desk waved Annie through.

As usual, Penny and her friends clustered around the exercise bikes. Annie's instructions were to not engage, but that didn't exclude getting close. The treadmills were near enough that she could overhear their conversation.

Lucy, the lady in the gray outfit who had lost her necklace, was back, working out on a cable machine. Annie considered going over and saying hi, but she had a job to do. Besides, it appeared the lady was wrapping up things.

Annie grabbed the treadmill's handrails for balance and started her warm-up stretches. It had been too long since she'd done them, and her muscles protested. Her physical therapist would have yelled at her.

Lucy headed towards the locker room. That would have escaped Annie's notice, except two of the bleached-blondes from Penny's group followed her. It didn't feel coincidental.

She should mind her own business.

The hell she would.

She pretended to be going to the front desk to throw off anyone watching her, then detoured to the dressing rooms. Before she silently opened the door partway, she heard loud voices.

Penny's friends hovered over Lucy, who was seated on the bench. "I paid my fees," she said.

"Not our cut." The speaker was the woman who had handed Penny the shiny object on Annie's last visit.

So, not only were they stealing members' personal items, they were shaking them down for money. Annie snapped a few pictures and wished she had a tape recorder. Right now, if she took it to the cops, it would be her word against theirs.

"I'm not giving you anything," Lucy tried to stand, but was pushed down by both of the Barbie wanna-be's.

Annie snapped a few more pictures and prayed the action was in the viewfinder.

"Where's your purse?" Barbie One demanded. "I bet you have a handful of credit cards. You won't mind if we borrow one or two, right?"

It was too much. Annie pushed the door open the rest of the way. "Is there a problem here?"

Three pairs of eyes widened.

"Oh, look," Barbie Two said. "Another newbie. This is our lucky day."

"You think so?" Annie smirked. She closed the door and put her back to it to prevent unwanted visitors. "You two look like a couple of newbies yourself. Either that, or you've learned everything you don't know by watching TV."

"You've got a smart mouth," Barbie One sneered. "Too bad you don't have a way to back it up."

Never underestimate the enemy. She jerked her head towards the far side of the room.

"Ma'am, there's a phone around the corner," she said. "May I suggest you call 911? Tell them it's for charges of attempted theft, extortion, and kidnapping."

"You're a cop?" Barbie One gasped.

"No way," Barbie Two snickered. "Bitches

like her can't be the fuzz."

How could she be so right and so wrong at the same time? Annie glanced around, looking for a weapon. She couldn't count on help from the elderly lady, who still sat, seemingly frozen, on the bench. Although her physical therapist had taught her a few self-defense skills after hearing stories about the divorce, she wasn't good enough to fight off both Barbies at the same time.

"Ma'am?" she said, deepening her voice, "Ma'am? The phone call?"

"Oh, yes." Lucy stood and pushed Barbie One out of the way, then disappeared around the corner.

"Let us out of here," Barbie Two said, raising her voice and her fists. Her tightly pulled back ponytail bounced as she took several threatening steps towards Annie.

Annie shifted her feet into a fighting stance, her weight on the balls of her feet. She had a weapon of sorts in her hands–her gym bag. It wouldn't damage anything, but would act as a shield.

Barbie One moved first. Annie wasn't sure exactly where the woman was heading, but couldn't let her leave. She aimed for Barbie One's middle and swung her bag—hard.

Her aim was true. Barbie One stumbled into the row of lockers. She'd have at least one major bruise on her back from the door handles, but Annie had no sympathy for her.

Lucy peeked around the corner and then disappeared. Annie hoped that meant she was keeping the police dispatcher updated and the cops would arrive soon. She figured that someone from Penny's group would come to check on her friends any time.

Barbie Two stood still, her eyes shifting between her friend and Annie.

"Make it easy on yourself." Annie positioned the gym bag to prepare it for a second round of action. "Have a seat and behave yourself until the cops get here. Maybe they'll cut you some slack."

That didn't happen. Annie hadn't expected it would. Barbie Two dove towards her. Annie sidestepped her and the woman collided with the door. Annie winced at the loud crack and watched as the woman slid to the floor. Had she broken something?

But Annie had made a mistake. She'd stopped paying attention to Barbie One. Something hard hit the back of her shoulders and she stumbled. She twisted to see a broom handle aimed at her face.

She raised an arm, ducked, and prayed. The handle smacked against Annie's arm and she dropped to her knees. If she didn't summon the strength to defend herself, she'd lose the battle.

Chapter Nine

Annie was out of tricks. Her gym bag, unreachable on the grimy floor of the locker room, offered nothing in the way of weapons. The scraps of paper that littered the concrete were of no use. Barbie One raised the broom, ready to strike again. An acrid taste flooded her mouth, reminding her of the days before the divorce, when Ian was at his worst; fear.

She wouldn't allow herself to be beaten like that ever again. From her kneeling position, she lunged forward and grabbed Barbie One by the calves. The force carried her opponent to the floor. That should put them on equal footing.

It wasn't her intention to hurt the woman; but she'd do what she had to. "Stay down, damn it," she hissed, "if you know what's good for you."

Naturally, Barbie One didn't pay attention. She twisted and wriggled. Annie resorted to laying on top of her and wrapped one arm around her neck and shoulders. It was like being a bareback rider on a bucking bronco. If Barbie Two rejoined the fight, there'd be no way for Annie to win the battle. Lucy wasn't of any help.

A loud bang on the locker room door caused Annie to lose her concentration, but she couldn't turn to check who was there. Her immediate worry was that Penny had arrived.

"Police!" a man's voice roared. "Nobody move!"

Annie rolled off her attacker and raised her hands to shoulder-height.

Annie wondered if she still had a job, because Coulson and Mike were in a deep discussion with the lead detective. Not Myers, thankfully. She would've loved to overhear the conversation, but she sat on the floor on the other side of the gym, her hands behind her back in cuffs. She couldn't do anything to relieve the dull ache between her shoulders where she'd been hit by the broom handle.

Annie leaned her head against the wall and closed her eyes. She'd be there whenever they decided what to do with her. Jail might be in her future. She didn't want to end up sharing a cell with Penny's friends, Vanessa and Linda. Penny had abandoned them in the exodus of the gym's customers when the cops arrived.

Footsteps crossed the room and stopped in front of her. She didn't open her eyes, recognizing the little hitch in the left step. "So, what's the verdict, Mike?"

He sat beside her. "You weren't supposed to approach."

"Penny," she corrected him. "I wasn't supposed to approach Penny. I didn't."

"What am I going to do with you, Ms. McGregor?"

"I didn't want anything to happen to that woman. She had nothing to do with any of this."

"Miriam Lucy Hinds. H-I-N-D-S. Not one of those Heinz's. That's the name of the lady you rescued."

Annie knew exactly who he was referring to. She opened her eyes. "Has either Vanessa or Linda ratted out Penny?"

"They crumbled like crackers the minute the detective started listing potential charges and jail times."

"What charges do I face?"

Mike made her wait. She deserved it. "Mrs. Hinds stuck up for you. It appears you're going to get off scot-free."

"Then why am I still in these cuffs?" Annie rattled them against the wall.

"I'm not sure. Something about waiting for official judgment from up the chain."

She studied a pile of dust on the floor. "In other words, despite Mrs. Hinds' statement, someone up the line has it in for me."

"That's one interpretation. But Detective Hills over there won't confirm or deny. Coulson is still arguing the decision."

"You guys got here awful quick. I don't trust that you both just happened to be in the neighborhood."

"Frank had a bad feeling. Coulson shared it with me. I always take steps to protect my people." Mike shifted a stray hair away from her mouth.

"It's a fine line between protecting and not trusting, Mike."

He was saved by Coulson coming their way.

"Good news," Coulson boomed. "The good detective has agreed to taking the cuffs off, Annie, although you aren't free to leave yet."

"Which of the suspects has the connections to delay her release?" Mike asked.

Coulson sat on the other side of Annie, making the space cramped. "The cops are covering their asses. Evidently, they've been receiving complaints about this location for weeks and they've been ignoring them. A lost necklace here, a few bucks cash there weren't worth their time and attention. Then our Annie comes along and makes them look bad."

Annie rolled her eyes. She wasn't anyone's Annie, but wouldn't argue with Coulson when she was at such a disadvantage. "So, they're punishing me."

"No, they are doing an in-depth investigation before they let anyone else slip away like Penny and Honey did." Coulson patted her knee. "Be patient."

"How did Honey know not to show up

today?" Annie asked.

"According to Detective Hills, she called out sick. She got lucky."

Speaking of Detective Hills, an older man with a hefty beer belly, he was coming their way. Annie hoped he brought the cufflink keys with him. He stopped in front of Annie, his feet planted firmly, as if he expected an attack. "You are being released, Mrs. McGregor, but we may need to talk with you again, so don't leave the area."

Annie struggled to stand. Simultaneously, Mile and Coulson each grabbed an elbow and carefully lifted her to an upright position. It took a moment for blood to rush back to her legs and to steady herself before she turned around to present her wrists to the cop.

Once the cuffs were off, Annie shook her arms and groaned. She needed an ice pack or two on her back and a hot bath.

"Are you okay?" Mike asked.

"I never considered a broom as a weapon," Annie said. "But she hit hard."

"Do you need medical assistance? We can bump the assault up to aggravated," the detective said.

"I'll take her to be checked after we're done here," Mike said. "You'll need pictures of her injuries."

"And I need to call Mr. Pearson," Coulson said, "before he goes home and finds his wife missing or she feeds him a pack of lies."

The old, three-story brick library had been her refuge more than once in her life. As a child, it was a magical place with more books than she'd ever be able to read and kind women who helped her find her next favorite one. During her marriage, it had been a hideout on Ian's bad days. Now, it was a safe place to work while healing and not having to worry about Mike hanging over her shoulder, worrying about her.

There was more to the Stanwich family than met the eye, but Annie couldn't figure out what she'd missed. And the few records she had found that included Kathleen didn't give her any clues. Mrs. Stanwich hadn't signed the service agreement yet, but Mike allowed Annie to keep researching the case to avoid assigning her to anything that might be dangerous. At least, that was Annie's theory.

But she'd promised Mike she'd work on the agency's book this afternoon. That would give her time to pick his brain on what she'd found.

"I need to

make a garbage run," she said as she studied a check from Mike's stack, trying to determine if the first figure was a four or a seven. The scrawled writing was as bad as a doctor's, and Annie couldn't decipher it.

"What are you hoping to find?" Mike asked from the other side of his desk.

"Bank statements. Nothing adds up. Mrs. Stanwich doesn't strike me as a person who would bother shredding them. I want to at least figure out what bank or banks she deals with. Mr. Stanwich died two years ago, and she's having problems paying you? Either he didn't leave a life insurance policy or she hasn't managed her money very well."

Mrs. Stanwich's original check had bounced. A teenage boy had come by with an envelope of cash to cover it, and pay for another hour of investigative time. Still no contract, though.

"I'll get Jorge to do it." He held a hand up to stave off Annie's protest. "Mrs. Stanwich knows your face. If you got caught, it would destroy the investigation. Jorge doesn't have that liability."

It made sense to Annie. "A bank statement won't give me a complete picture, but it'll give me a starting point."

"What are you hoping to find?"

"Where her money is coming from and going to. Her entire story doesn't make sense.

Why has it taken this long for her to search for her daughter after her husband's death? By the way, those were fake tears she cried at the meeting."

Mike crunched his mouth. "I thought so, but wasn't sure. Old ladies' tears are my Kryptonite."

She grinned. "Good to know."

"Oh, no." Mike shook his finger at her. "You aren't going to get off that easy. Now that you know, you'll be my lead shield."

Annie rolled her eyes. "That's not in my job description."

"Who wrote your job description?" he asked with an arch of his eyebrows.

He was teasing her? This was a side of Mike Annie hadn't seen before. It made her uncomfortable, like a barrier had been lifted, and she wasn't ready to deal with the possibilities. "I get it. You're the boss, despite Coulson's ambitions."

"Speaking of, I heard from him. Penny has been located at a friend's house. Mr. Pearson has started the paperwork for a divorce. You may need to testify for that as well as the criminal case. You'll be paid for your time, of course."

She'd spent enough time in courtrooms during her own divorce and hoped the Pearsons would settle their case without involving her. She didn't have much hope that would happen.

"When is Jorge going to raid Mrs.

Stanwich's garbage?" she asked, returning to the original topic.

"I've left that up to Jorge. He'll do it when the time is right. I trust him."

Did that mean he didn't trust her, Annie wondered, as she picked up the next check on the pile.

With the Hansens out of town for a few more days, it seemed the perfect opportunity to stop by the video store Bobby Hansen had visited. Annie didn't expect to get any solid information; it was more for gathering background information.

An old-fashioned bell rang when Annie pushed open the door. It was exactly what she had anticipated–the dingy yellow walls and several rows of wooden shelves filled with black video cases. Although there were categories denoted by signs on the top of the racks, a quick glance showed that many of the movies were in the wrong place.

Annie nodded to the old man who came out from the back room and sat on a stool behind the front counter. Most of the movies were several years old and appealed to a younger audience. Still, she browsed the limited selection.

She spotted an open doorway covered by

a curtain in the right-hand corner, and a sign overhead that read 'adults only.' She assumed that's where they kept their porn offerings. The titles they rented out must not have had much appeal, based on the lack of customers. How did the owners make any money?

Unless the operation was a cover for an illegal operation. Drug sales would be an easy guess, but again, Annie spotted nothing to support that conclusion. She wondered if the owners used it as an income tax deduction.

Annie decided there wasn't any reason for her to stick around. It's not like she could ask the old man about Hansen. Without sparing him another glance, she left the store, the bell ringing cheerfully behind her.

She sat in her truck for a few minutes, deciding her next step. She didn't want to go back to her apartment. It had been her refuge for over a year, but now that it was fully furnished, it felt cramped. Or she'd just outgrown it. But the neighborhood bar around the corner remained welcoming, and that's where she headed. A good way to start the weekend.

Chapter Ten

Annie had stopped paying attention to the cheers and groans of the other bar patrons as they reacted to the Pirates game on the TV. As hard as she tried, she could never work up the commitment to the local team. She buried herself in a drugstore romance novel, nibbled on peanuts, and sipped her beer, only looking up when the cheers were especially loud.

"You never change, do you, bitch?" a man's voice said.

It was the voice of her nightmares. Annie closed her book, took a deep breath, and prepared for the confrontation. "Go away, Ian."

"Not a chance. You owe me, and I'm here to collect."

Her gun was in her purse and the bar too crowded to use it safely. She studied her ex and mentally listed what else she had at hand that could be used as a weapon. Prison hadn't done him any favors. His boyish good looks were gone, replaced with the face of a man with too many scars and pockmarks. The crude crucifix tattoo on his neck didn't help.

To even the playing field, Annie slid out of the chair and stood, her feet planted slightly apart, ready for action. She didn't have time to settle in before Ian pulled back his arm. She anticipated what was coming, having been on the receiving end of his fist too many times.

Her swivel wasn't fast enough. His knuckles grazed her cheek, and she staggered back a step. The old Annie would have crumpled. This Annie didn't. She balled her hands together and swung. It was liberating. She'd never fought back.

Annie kept her desk lamp turned off and tried to work by the limited light that filtered through the front window. Betty was the only other person in the office; but everyone else would stream in soon for the weekly staff meeting. She should have called in sick, but didn't want to stay home. The cops hadn't caught up to Ian yet.

She immersed herself in going through Mrs. Stanwich's documents, hoping to find something she'd missed. As each of the guys drifted in, she'd give them a quick wave, but turned her face away from them. She'd hoped it would be good enough.

Mike, in a rare event, was the last one in and headed straight to his office. Annie wondered what the problem was, but it wasn't her business. She kept her head down and focused on the task at hand. When Mike's footsteps crossed the room and stopped in front of her desk, she knew her ploy hadn't worked.

"Look at me," he ordered.

Reluctantly, she raised her head.

He reached down and turned on her desk lamp. "The makeup helps, but not enough to fool me. Or any of the four investigators you work with. Who did this, Annie?"

She fought the urge to rub her cheek. There was no use in lying. "I had a run-in with my ex. He sucker punched me when I tried to leave his exalted presence. But no worries, he probably looks worse than me. He picked the wrong place for the confrontation."

Jorge walked over and put his palms on her desk. "When did this happen?"

"And where?" Ric, another of Mike's staff, asked.

"Where is your ex now?" Denny cracked his knuckles.

"What happened?" Mike asked.

"Friday, I stopped for a drink at Moe's, around the corner from my apartment complex. It's a little neighborhood joint, nothing fancy. That's when he showed up. I don't know how he found me. Anyway, the restraining order against him had expired. Not that a piece of paper would have stopped him."

"You fought him off?" Jorge asked, admiration in his voice.

"Not by myself. My ex didn't do his homework. The retired vets that hang out at the bar weren't happy with someone coming in and disturbing their chill evening. They especially didn't appreciate him hurting me. They've adopted me as their daughter."

"And where is he now?" Ric put a hand on her shoulder.

"I can't say. Once the guys made sure he wasn't going to punch me again, and I'd gotten a few good jabs, they focused on me and he took off before the cops showed up."

The scene had been almost comical. As Ian had raised his right arm to hit her again, Sam had grabbed it. Ace had grabbed his other arm, and Cap'n had used his wheelchair as a battering ram, keeping Ian off-balance while Annie found her footing and had thrown a few of her own punches. Enough damage had been done to him to get the message across. She wasn't an easy target anymore.

Annie continued, "It took a while for the cops to show up. Kenny, the bartender, had fixed me up with an ice pack and the boys and I had almost finished the first round of free beers before the cops strolled in."

"I don't like to interfere in my employees' lives," Mike said, his voice deeper than normal, "But I'm going to this time. I need all the info you have on your ex. A picture, his address, where he works, whatever you can come up with. If we work together, we can find him."

"I haven't kept track of him since the

divorce." Annie hadn't seen him since he'd slithered into her hospital room asking for a loan. Thankfully, the charge nurse had tossed him out. "Obviously, he's kept tabs on me since he knew where I hang out. Time to move again."

"No." Annie turned to see Denny, the quiet one, clenching and unclenching his fists. "You do that, and he wins the battle. We stop this here and now, no matter what. We'll do it legally, of course. But your ex won't know what hit him. Between the five of us, we have connections he can't imagine. We can make his life hell."

"She can stay in my guest room," Betty said from around the corner, where her desk was.

Mike shook his head. "Nope. I won't put you on the radar of Annie's ex. We'll get a hotel for her for a few days. On the company's account."

Annie hoped it would be better than the one she'd spent the weekend in. She'd picked it on price alone. The room had come with a few bugs as roommates.

"We'll schedule shifts to guard her," Jorge said. "If we include Coulson and his guys, we'll still have time to work our cases."

"I'm sitting right here," Annie said dryly. "How about asking me for my input? I'm a professional too, remember?"

She hadn't expected the bodyguard duties to follow her to the library, Owen, Coulson's sleight-of-hand expert, sat at a nearby library table with a stack of newspapers in front of him while she scrolled through microfiche information about the Stanwich's. She hoped, but didn't expect, to find something she'd missed in her earlier research. Annie still didn't have any clues about what happened to Kathleen. Mrs. Stanwich hadn't come through with more information or a signed contract, but Mike had okay'd Annie spending more time working the case. The library provided a safe space. Annie doubted Ian had ever entered a library.

Owen stood, stretched, and meandered over to Annie. "Lunchtime," he announced, standing in a spot that blocked Annie's view of the front door.

"It's only a quarter after eleven," she protested.

"Your two hours are up."

Annie leaned back and rubbed her eyes. "It's time I took a break, I guess."

"I'm supposed to escort you to Coulson's office. Mike is concerned that your ex is watching his agency, and doesn't want to establish any set pattern for your comings and goings."

Annie gathered up the films to return to the desk. "Or we should use me as bait to draw him out."

"The bosses are in charge, not us," Owen grinned. "We'll play by their rules—for now."

Owen had also acted as her chauffeur, so they took his little Ford Escort to the Nation, Inc. office. Annie spent her time watching the mirrors, keeping an eye out for anyone following them, but their path appeared to be clear. She'd almost hoped they'd run into Ian, so she could deal with him and get him out of her life again.

They took a long, circuitous route, though areas of town Annie wasn't familiar with. They were stopped at an intersection when a familiar car drove past. Annie put her hand on Owen's arm. "Follow that car."

"Your ex?" he asked.

"No. A case that has been frustrating me for weeks. Bobby Hansen. He's supposed to be out of town."

"What's the story?" Owen made the left after two more cars went by.

"The typical. Cheating. I haven't been able to catch him. But I'm positive he's up to something."

"Well, let's see where he goes." He picked up a walkie-talkie and pushed the button. "Owl to base," he said. "Owl to base. We're taking a detour. There's no sign of the fox, but something else interesting popped up."

"Roger. Stay safe."

Annie didn't recognize the voice at the other end, but she hadn't met all of Coulson's people.

"And out," Owen responded.

Bobby signaled for a right-hand turn, and Owen followed. The neighborhood looked familiar, and she tried to figure out why. Then Bobby made another right into a small strip mall, and the light went on. The Chinese restaurant she'd followed him to before.

"Just drive by," she told Owen. "I don't want to show up where he can get a good look at my face."

"Fair enough. My specialty is short-term work. But I could go in and pick up some take-out." Still, he drove down the street.

"Another time. I don't want to make Mike nervous."

"Or Coulson?" Owen asked with a smirk.

"He's not my problem."

"He'd like to be."

Annie huffed. "That's all I need. Another complication in my life."

Owen laughed. "We'll keep him away from you as much as possible. It's not the first time we've run interference. Sometimes we're protecting him, sometimes the object of his attentions."

"And occasionally both?"

"That happens." They merged onto a major street and headed towards Coulson's office. Owen checked his rear and sideview mirrors. "Still clear."

They got to the office about ten minutes later. Lunch, an assortment of sandwiches, waited for them in the breakroom. Owen grabbed a sandwich and left, leaving Annie alone. It wasn't long before Coulson shambled in.

He stopped in front of Annie, and coughed. She couldn't ignore him without being rude, so she looked up. He studied her face and nodded. "I thought it would be worse. You must have avoided most of the blow."

"I didn't duck fast enough." Annie rubbed her cheek. The bruise was fading, but her makeup only partially disguised it.

"Mike reports that no one has any leads to your ex's location. And his last known address with his parole officer was an apartment that is now occupied by a family of five."

"He's probably holed up and nursing his wounds. Won't show his face until the fuss dies down. If he follows his normal pattern, he's plotting his next attack."

"I need a list of his friends. People that would hide him." Coulson pulled a small notepad from a pocket and picked up a pen lying on the table.

"He didn't let me meet his friends and accused me of flirting with them." He'd also claimed she'd flirted with her own brother and used it to isolate her from her family and friends.

"Where does he hang out?"

"Like the woman he was cheating with,

his favorite bar changed every few weeks." Annie blinked back the tears. The physical scars would fade, but would the mental scars heal?

Coulson crouched in front of her. "Lord knows I'm not good at this empathy stuff, but listen to me, Annie. You may not realize how strong you are, but you've beat the odds more than once. We're all rooting for you to do it again."

"He'll never let me live my life in peace. He believes he owns me."

"I've worked enough divorce cases to recognize the type. I'd rather work insurance fraud, any day. There's rarely a satisfactory ending in a case like yours. You can be the exception, Annie. In a way, you'll redeem all of us."

"No pressure," Annie laughed shakily. "I'm no superhero. Don't expect too much."

"Just be patient with us. You've been working with Mike long enough to realize these things take time. We'll do our best to stay out of your way while making sure you stay safe."

"The easiest thing to do would be to set me up as bait."

"Mike and I talked about it as a last resort." Coulson stood. "It's not time yet."

"I used to think I was a patient person. This job has taught me otherwise. I'm used to seeing immediate results in accounting, and investigating is a slow process." Annie wrapped her leftovers in a napkin and set it aside. She'd lost what little appetite she'd had.

"When you're ready, Frank will take you back to Mike's office." Coulson paused, then reached out and put a hand on her shoulder. "But you're welcome to stay here."

Annie wasn't sure if he was being supportive or something more. It had been a long time since a man had been interested in her. She no longer recognized the difference between friendly conversation and flirting. With Coulson's reputation, she couldn't risk getting involved in anything personal.

She took the easy way out. "I'll hitch a ride with Frank."

Chapter Eleven

"The wait is getting to me, Mike. I'd like to have my life back." Annie held the binoculars to her eyes and scanned the windows of the house down the street. They sat in his car, waiting for the cleaning lady to drag the garbage can to the alley and leave. Mrs. Stanwich hadn't produced any of the documents Annie had asked for. No school records for Kathleen, no contacts for friends, not even a yearbook. Mike had suggested her first garbage excursion. Annie suspected it was a way for him to keep an eye on her.

The home was a two-story colonial, one of several cookie-cutter houses that lined the street. Unlike the other homes, Mrs. Stanwich's yard needed attention, and the untrimmed hedges would provide cover for their expedition without waiting until darkness fell. Mrs. Stanwich was out with her bridge club buddies, according to the phone conversation Mike had with her the previous day.

"It's only been thirty minutes," Mike grinned.

"That's not what I mean, and you know it. It's been a week. You'd think there'd be some sign of Ian by now. He wasn't good at being sneaky."

"And this is where I'm supposed to give you a speech about these things taking time. But I won't, because you've heard it before. It bothers me that your ex hasn't shown his face. He must have made new friends in jail and he's holed up with one of them. I don't have the right connections to get that information." Mike drummed his fingers on the steering wheel.

Annie leaned forward and raised the binoculars again. "It looks like a go. She just rolled the can out."

"Soon. If the info I have is correct, she walks down to the bus stop three blocks away."

"That's a long walk after a hard day spent cleaning."

"Especially in the winter," Mike blew on his fingers and rubbed his hands together.

"Two of those blocks are uphill." It was only half a joke. Everywhere in old Pittsburgh was either up or down. Out in this part of town, the hills flattened out.

"Both ways. With no shoes on."

Was Mike cracking a joke? This was a side to him Annie hadn't seen before. "Did your dad use that line on you, too?"

"The first major snowstorm of each year. He usually only tried it once a season."

"My dad used it every chance he got. It got so bad that my brother and me started quoting his words back at him after the first sentence."

Annie studied the other backyards along the alley. No one had claimed a spot to trim flowers or work on a suntan. "How did you get the info on the cleaner's schedule, Mike?"

"Ric did a spot of side work for me. Normally, the PI assigned to the case would handle it, but I didn't want to take a chance on Mrs. Stanwich seeing your face."

"And there she goes." Annie reached for the box of plastic gloves in the back seat. "I don't know if I'm looking forward to this or dreading it."

Mike took the pair of gloves she handed him. "It's a crapshoot. With a little luck, you'll find what you need on top. But don't count on it."

Mrs. Stanwich's garbage looks nothing like mine, Annie thought, opening the last of the black garbage bags. Only one of them held kitchen trash. The lady either ate out most of the time or didn't eat much of anything at all. Considering Mrs. Stanwich's physique, Annie didn't believe that for a second.

"You finding anything?" she asked Mike.

He shook his head. "Nothing. That's the way it works sometimes."

Annie spotted shredded paper in her bag. So much for a golden opportunity. But she had to go all the way, so she dug deeper, pushing aside a stack of newspapers. And struck gold. Or at least a stack of undestroyed sheets. "Success!" she proclaimed and held them up.

One side of Mike's lips rose. "Don't get cocky. That may be a bunch of ads. We'll head back to the office and find out."

Annie closed the bag and returned the garbage to the can. Owen had warned her Mike didn't allow them to leave a mess behind. Something about an old Boy Scout rule and leaving a place cleaner than when you started. With that in mind, she gathered up a few discarded cigarette butts and added them to the can before Mike put the lid back on. He nodded and Annie took it as a sign of approval.

She realized how much his approval meant to her as she waded through the papers later. Most of them were useless, decades old correspondence from her alma mater. Mrs. Stanwich must have cleaned out some old storage boxes from the attic or garage. Annie set aside the stack of Kathleen's schoolwork to examine later. Why had it been in the trash? Didn't the woman value it as a keepsake?

She focused on a bank statement from several months earlier, torn in quarters, but not shredded. Tape would fix that.

The overhead lights flickered, and Annie looked up to see Mike and Denny by the light switch. Since Mike had moved her desk and put up a room partition, she no longer had a window view and easily lost track of the time of day.

"Time to go home," Mike said.

"I was just getting to the good stuff," she protested.

"It'll still be here tomorrow," Denny smiled. "Or take it with you. A little bedtime reading."

Mike raised an eyebrow. "I don't expect my people to work on their own time."

Annie snorted. "You set a fine example."

"Considering the job requires a lot of night work, that's meaningless." Denny winked at Annie. "Don't pretend any of us lives a normal life. None of us want to sit behind a desk and work a 9-5. That includes you, Annie."

He was right. She had never imagined her career to be anything but desk work, but she was enjoying her new life. Mostly, anyway. Once the problem of Ian was resolved, things would be much better. Annie gathered up the papers.

"Let's do this, Denny," she said. "Supper's on me."

The mom-and-pop diner didn't have the fanciest food in the world. The furnishings were old and worn, but the prices were cheap. Besides, Mom and Pop, the elderly couple who owned the restaurant, treated regular customers like family. They eyed Denny with interest and seemed disappointed when Annie introduced him as a coworker. Still, his plate of rigatoni seemed to be piled higher than usual.

"Does your ex know about this place?" Denny asked between bites. He and Annie sat in a booth halfway towards the back. He monitored the street entrance while Annie tracked the kitchen doors.

"No, the rehab staff used to bring me here as part of my therapy." At the startled look on Denny's face, she hastened to explain. "Not that kind of rehab. After the accident, I had to learn to walk again."

Denny reached over the table and patted her hand. "I was aware you'd had medical issues, but Mike never revealed what they were. Your therapists did a great job because your limp is hardly noticeable."

Even Mike didn't know how bad her condition had been. "Wait until this winter. The cold and snow will slow me down."

"I've got a weathervane elbow from an old football injury." Denny flexed his arm. "I understand."

A man walked by them, headed for the restroom. Annie stiffened and leaned forward. "Did you see his face?" she hissed.

"That wasn't your ex."

"No. You remember the Bobby Hansen

case?" She'd studied Hansen from both the front and from behind, and that ass looked familiar.

"That's been dropped, right?" Denny asked.

Annie nodded. "Temporarily, at least. But it's a heck of a coincidence that he's here. Where was he sitting? Is he alone?"

"I wasn't paying attention. The question is, did he spot you?"

"He'll have a better chance when he comes back." She put her purse on the table. If nothing else, she could pretend to be searching it to hide her face.

"No women are sitting by themselves." Denny shifted to get a different angle of sight. "That doesn't eliminate the possibility that he's part of a group."

Annie turned her head towards the wall as Bobby re-emerged from the restroom, but used a mirror she'd pulled from her purse to keep track until he passed by. She jerked her head in his direction and Denny nodded.

"He sat with another man," Denny said in a soft voice, twisting in his seat. "Short brown hair, clean shaven, average weight, can't tell much more about him since he's seated. If I had to guess, they're business acquaintances, that's all."

"Another dead end." Annie shook her head. "No matter what his wife thinks, I can't find any proof he's cheating. Maybe they're having a rough time and he doesn't like to spend time at home."

"But you don't believe that."

"No. Still, there's nothing solid to present to Mrs. Hansen. Mike keeps telling me that it happens that way sometimes, but it's hard to give up." She quirked her mouth and returned her attention to her pasta.

They waited for Hansen to leave before they left and Denny took her home. At her apartment, a third-floor, one bedroom place in an old brick building, Annie stood in the doorway, shifting from foot to foot, while Denny searched the apartment. She'd conceded to the procedure after a long discussion with Mike. But something was off and she couldn't put her finger on it.

"All clear," Denny said, coming out of her bedroom.

She hesitated. "Can you stick around while I look?"

"What's wrong?"

With a sniff, she stepped inside. "It smells funny. Like a man's aftershave. Not yours. The door was locked, right?"

"Yes. I checked. Could your landlord have come in to make repairs?"

"He lives out-of-state somewhere. The maintenance company has an office west of town."

She set her purse on the sofa she'd

bought at a second-hand store a few blocks away. It had bare spots she kept covered with a multi-colored crocheted throw her grandmother had made. Not that she ever had guests over to sit on it. Annie pulled her revolver from the purse. "This will only take a minute."

There weren't many places for an average-sized person to hide. Holding her gun at her side, she opened every cupboard and peeked behind each piece of furniture, then headed for the bedroom.

Denny trailed behind her. "Anything out of place?" he asked.

She scanned the room. Nothing appeared to be touched, but the scent seemed stronger. And there were wrinkles in the bedspread that she would never have left. She backed up, bumping into Denny. "He was in here."

"He, who?"

She spun around. "I assume Ian. Laying on my bed was his way of leaving the message that I can't escape him. If he stayed true to form, he left a note where I'd find it when I went to bed."

"We won't wait that long." He pushed by her, grabbed the bedspread and shook it out, then methodically stripped her bed. She grabbed her pillows and pulled the covers off. Nothing fluttered to the floor.

She shoved her revolver into the front of her waistband, set her hands on her hips, and studied the room, trying to remember other spots Ian had used. More than once, he'd scribbled on the boxes of her personal products or on a roll of toilet paper. She hoped that wouldn't be the case now—it would be embarrassing if Denny found a note in either place.

"Check your dresser drawers," Denny suggested.

That was her next step. Annie didn't look forward to going through her underwear drawer while he watched. Ian once put an obscenity-filled note inside her favorite pair of panties. At least her underwear was of the boring variety these days, nothing Denny wouldn't have seen before.

Her hands shook as she opened the dresser. Without even checking, Annie saw that half the items were missing. "Damn it. He left me a message, all right. I wonder what else he took."

"Do you keep any money stashed?"

Her pitiful emergency fund was well-hidden, but she wasn't sure if it was hidden enough to keep it out of Ian's sticky fingers. She also kept a jar of loose change on the TV stand. It was mostly pennies and nickels, but she hoped he'd found that and not looked any deeper. "In the freezer," she said. "In a block of ice in a bag of frozen vegetables. If he took it, he'll have to work hard to get to it, or wait. Patience was never his strong point. And he hates peas."

Denny chuckled. "I like your intricate thought process. Hope it worked."

There was one way to find out. On the way to the kitchen, Annie wondered if her other hiding spot had been detected. It took a Phillips-head screwdriver to remove the cover on the heating duct.

"Well, he ate the rest of my chocolate-chip cookies," she said, seeing the empty package in the garbage can. "They were almost gone, anyway."

She opened the freezer and spotted the bag of peas on the bottom shelf. As soon as she picked up the package, she knew her money was safe. "It's still here. I can tell by the weight."

"Good. Now go pack a bag. You can't stay here tonight."

"And go where? I don't have money for a decent hotel for more than a night or two. And that's when I get my stash thawed out." Annie hefted the bag of peas.

"I'll give Mike a call and we'll figure it out." Denny glanced around the front room. "Where's your phone?"

"On the end table by the couch," Annie said. She turned and pointed, then dropped her hand. "At least, it was there. Why would he steal the phone?"

Chapter Twelve

"The phone isn't even worth pawning. It was the cheapest one available." Annie picked up the wire leading to the jack in the front room of her apartment. She'd washed the wall when she'd moved in, but the white paint had yellowed from the gas heat fumes. "Why would Ian take it?"

"To keep you from calling for help?" Denny asked.

"Which means he's coming back." She fought the bile that rose in her throat. No matter how long it had been, the fear Ian had ingrained in her would never go away.

"Either that, or he's hiding nearby, hoping you go to the phone booth down the block." Denny drew his gun from his shoulder holster, checked that the chamber was loaded, and the safety engaged.

Her ex had proven he could get access to her apartment anytime. Why wait for her to leave? "He doesn't have the patience for that."

"I don't understand his motivation." Denny scratched his head.

"Anything he can do to annoy me," Annie suggested.

"Annoying is prank calls. Not punching you in the face and breaking into your apartment."

"The abuse warped my standards."

"That doesn't make it better. Go pack. You need to go. Now."

Arguing with Denny was pointless. Annie dug her beat-up suitcase out of the closet and started neatly folding clothes to put in it.

She took a deep-blue blouse off its hanger and ran her hand over the silk-like material. Annie had worn it at her bridal shower. She'd felt like a princess that day, but things hadn't worked out the way she'd hoped. She'd lost touch with most of her friends after the wedding.

A loud crash in the front room brought Annie back to earth. She tossed the blouse on her bed. "Denny? Everything okay?"

Denny didn't answer. Annie hesitated for a moment before yanking her weapon from her waistband, praying she wouldn't need it. With safety procedures whirling in her brain, she assumed the proper stance and stepped out of her bedroom into the short hallway.

"Sorry, I dropped a stack of books," Denny called.

She leaned against the wall and took a moment to collect her nerves before slipping the gun back into its spot. "I hope the bookmarks didn't fall out. I'd hate to lose my places."

"The Fall of Jake Hennessey?" Denny asked as she entered the front room.

Annie shrugged. "I spotted it in a second-hand store. It looked interesting. I haven't started it yet."

"You should take it with you. I suspect Mike is going to want to tuck you away for a few days."

"I'll fight Mike every step of the way. Ian had found my apartment, which means he'll find me anywhere." Still, she slid the book and two others into her suitcase.

Denny insisted on carrying it to his car. Daylight was fading, and streetlights flickered. Through the gaps between brick buildings, Annie caught glimpses of the setting sun. Crickets sang, and fireflies glimmered in the bushes. Under other circumstances, she would have enjoyed the beauty of the night.

Annie paid no attention to the footsteps behind them. They weren't the only ones out enjoying the evening. Then someone lit a firecracker. Denny stumbled. He dropped the suitcase and fell forward. A red stain spread across his back. Out of pure instinct, Annie reached for her weapon.

She switched off the safety as she spun around. Annie's gaze locked onto a scruffy man pointing a revolver at Denny. The click of a trigger and the scream of the attacker broke her from her trance. The man—not Ian—dropped to the sidewalk, his blood mingling with Denny's. She lowered her weapon. "Call the cops! Someone call 911!"

Denny had been taken to the nearest hospital and was in surgery. He'd been shot with a small caliber gun with a silencer. The attacker was in the same hospital, but his outlook wasn't as good as Denny's. Annie couldn't muster the empathy to care.

She rotated her shoulders, wishing she could lie down, close her eyes, and sleep the nightmare away. But the hard metal chair and cold table wouldn't let that happen. The cops kept popping in every few minutes to keep her awake. Besides, she was waiting for Mike and his lawyer to show up.

The doorknob rotated. Metal screeched against metal as the door opened. Annie expected one of the uniformed officers, but Detective Myers strode in, followed by Mike. He must have called in a favor to be allowed in the interview room instead of watching the procedures from outside.

"You are a thorn in my side, Mrs. McGregor," Myers growled.

Annie relied on her right to remain silent. It seemed to be the best option.

Myers waited only a few seconds before moving on. "What do you want to tell me about tonight?"

"You don't have to say anything," Mike

reminded her.

"How is Denny doing?" she asked.

"I haven't had an update."

"I don't understand why Denny was shot instead of me."

"Why would you be a target?" Myers asked, clicking his pen.

"My ex got out of prison a few weeks ago. We've already had one run-in. I assumed it was him who broke into my apartment today."

His eyebrows arched. "Do we have a report on that?"

"No. Denny wanted to get me somewhere safe first. Besides, my phone was taken in the break-in." Annie rubbed her temples.

"Anything else stolen?" Myers scribbled in the notepad he'd brought with him.

Heat rose in her cheeks. "About half of my underwear. I didn't dig any deeper."

"What proof do you have it was your ex? What's his name?"

"Ian. Ian McGregor. And I have no proof. But it's a logical assumption."

Myers scrunched his mouth. "There's nothing logical about you or this situation. And I don't see how it's related to you shooting the victim tonight."

Mike interrupted. "Your characterization of the victim may be skewed, Detective. Denny and Annie are the victims."

"Mrs. McGregor is the only person in the

encounter who wasn't injured," the detective pointed out.

"If she hadn't had a gun, both she and Denny might be dead," Mike countered. "What do the witnesses say?"

"The street cops are still working on it." Myers rolled his eyes. "The locals won't talk to me. They don't trust any cops except the ones they see regularly."

Which was why Annie had never disclosed her profession to her neighbors. As long as they thought she was nothing but a bookkeeper, they were willing to accept her. Now that she had betrayed that acceptance, would they turn their backs on her? Or would the story of her abusive ex be enough for her to not be cast out?

"Are you going to release Annie?" Mike asked. "She acted in self-defense."

Myers shook his head. "She'd be better off in protective custody until we can ID the man she shot and figure out how he is or isn't tied to her ex."

That bothered Annie, too, but she stuck with the silence is golden philosophy. Mike was doing a fine job of supporting her.

"I can arrange for Annie to leave town for several weeks," Mike suggested. "It'll give us time to track down her ex."

"I can't leave," Annie protested, finally speaking. "That would put you down two employees until Denny heals up.”

“Leave? I should put you in a holding cell with the hookers and druggies. You shot someone, McGregor,” Myers snorted.

The forty-five minutes Annie spent in the processing area had been more than enough time for Annie to know she didn’t want to spend anymore time than necessary in custody.

“I’d love to see you explain to the press why a heroic bookkeeper is being held on unknown charges.” Mike leaned back and crossed his arms. “At least two reporters have been notified of the incident.”

Myers pushed his metal chair away from the table and half-stood, to bring his face close to Mike’s. “Are you trying to blackmail me?”

“No, just apprising you of the facts.”

Annie retreated to her cone of silence. This was a power struggle between the two men, and Mike seemed to be winning.

“Don’t push me, Edwards. I can bury McGregor so deep in the system none of your contacts will be able to help her.”

“You’re a good cop, Myers. Your ethics won’t let you do that.”

The detective collapsed back into his chair. “I’ve looked into your background, Edwards, and I don’t understand why you left the department. I don’t like being on the other side, but this is your warning—don’t push me too far. And keep McGregor out of trouble.”

"I can't make any promises until we get her ex off the streets." Mike's eyes narrowed. "The cops don't seem to take his previous attack on Annie seriously."

"We have more important things to worry about." Myers frowned. "The figures for murder rates and rapes are down, but there are still too many of them. One parolee who isn't reporting in isn't our priority."

It was her priority, Annie thought, and she needed to stop relying on Mike and the rest of the guys to do all the footwork.

After knocking on the door, a uniformed cop walked in and laid a folded-up piece of paper in front of the detective. Myers turned so when he opened it, neither Annie nor Mike could read it.

"The man you shot has been identified," he said. "His street name was Lucky Propizo. He had a rap sheet a mile long. Mostly small-time crimes."

"Was?" Annie asked.

"After he got out of surgery, he had a heart attack. Nothing related to the injury. He's dead. Which is a stroke of luck for you, because I can't imagine the DA taking an interest in the case now."

"I didn't want him to die," Annie said under her breath.

Not softly enough. "You didn't kill him," Myers pointed out. "The amount of drugs he'd used in his lifetime was enough to do that."

So why did she feel guilty?

"The bad thing," Mike said, "is that we won't be able to question him and find out if he had ties to Annie's ex or if the attack was random."

The only luxury Mike had installed in the office building was the shooting range in the basement. It was used by not only the employees of the Edwards and Nation agencies, but occasionally by cops who were friends of Mike's. Painted gray to match the cinder blocks, it had space for three booths. The soundproofing and safety features were top-notch, and from the office upstairs, there was no sign the range existed. That morning, Annie had the space to herself.

But she wasn't shooting. She stood in the middle booth, holding her revolver with the proper form, but not pulling the trigger. She couldn't. In her imagination, Lucky's contorted face when the bullet hit him stared back at her from the target.

Would Mike despise her when she quit? She could stay on as a bookkeeper, but the part-time wages wouldn't be enough to support herself on. Annie hated the idea of leaving Mike in the lurch when Denny would be out of action for several weeks.

She put the revolver on the counter and then her hands, palms down, and leaned forward. A few stray tears followed, one splashing off the gun. Lucky may have been unlucky enough to have had a heart attack; but Annie blamed herself for his death. She wouldn't be able to shoot someone else, even if a situation demanded it.

The stress and lack of sleep were too much, and tears fell freely. When the basement door squeaked open, Annie swiped them from her cheeks and eyes.

"What are you doing?" Mike asked.

Annie panicked, not having an excuse. "Cleaning my gun." It was the first thing that came to mind.

He pushed past her and picked up her revolver. "Where's your cleaning kit?"

In her desk. She said nothing.

He returned the gun to the counter and stepped back. "Pick it up, Annie."

She'd forced herself to do that earlier, but Annie still had to stop her hands from trembling as she wrapped her fingers around the grip of the revolver. The next steps were instinctive-—checking the safety and ensuring a round was seated in the chamber.

Mike put on a set of earmuffs. "I'm waiting."

No need to ask for what. Annie assumed

the proper stance, unlocked the safety, and raised the weapon. The target hung right where it was supposed to. Just black ink on a yellow backboard. She put her finger on the trigger.

Then set the gun down. "I can't do it, Mike."

Chapter Thirteen

Annie stared at a fly on the ceiling. How had it made its way to the basement? "Give me half an hour and I'll type up my resignation."

Mike blocked her from leaving. "Turn around and stare at the target."

"Mike . . ."

"Trust me. Do it, Annie."

She faced the target, Lucky's face floating over the center.

Mike stepped closer. "What do you see?"

She sucked in a breath. "His face."

"Lucky's?"

"Yes."

"Look again," Mike ordered. "Focus on the bullseye."

Annie blinked. "The dot?"

He put his hands on her shoulders. "Yes."

She didn't understand why, but she did as he ordered. The large black spot wavered and settled.

"Keep your eye on the target and pick up your weapon."

Annie didn't want to disappoint him. She felt around on the counter until she found the gun's handle, repeating an exercise she'd completed during one of her training sessions.

"Keep your eye on the target, and tell me

if the safety is on," Mike said.

"It is," she answered after a moment.

"Release it and raise your weapon."

She reverted to acting on instinct, clicked off the safety, and sighted down the barrel. Annie didn't flinch as she squeezed the trigger.

The recoil didn't shake her. Her nose twitched at the acrid odor of burnt gunpowder, but otherwise she didn't move. She'd done this countless times. She waited for the length of two breaths, returned her gun to the counter, and pushed the button to bring the target up to the station.

It wasn't a perfect placement, but her shot had skimmed the edge of the bullseye. Pride warred with regret. "I killed a man, Mike."

"You heard Myers. Lucky had a heart attack. Besides, it was a choice between him and Denny. Which would you choose?"

"Denny, of course. But that doesn't make me feel any better." The tears she'd been holding back threatened to explode. "What if I can't squeeze the trigger the next time?"

"That's a challenge every one of us faces each time we pull our weapons."

Annie took off her headset and sniffed as she swiveled to face Mike. They were close enough that she could feel his breath on her face. "Have you had to do this for anyone else?"

He reached out and tucked a loose lock of hair behind her ear. "Yes. Then I took them out and got them drunk. I can't take that risk with you. Not now. Not with your ex still roaming the streets."

"I'll take a raincheck." It might be fun to go drinking with Mike. See what he was like once he'd loosened up a bit. Annie bet he knew all the right "wrong" places.

"I'll give it to you. In the meantime, I'm still working on how to get you out of town."

"Don't. Running away won't fix the problem." Annie forced a grin. "Unless there's a job in Wyoming. I've always wanted to go there."

"I don't have any connections that far west." Mike rubbed his chin. "Wyoming. eh? As in Cheyenne? Like your name?"

Annie nodded. He got it in one. "My parents met there. I've always wanted to check it out."

"I'd send you there on vacation, but the agency doesn't have the money." He grinned. "You would look good in a cowboy hat."

She'd owned one, once upon a time. Ian had destroyed it and she'd never bought a replacement. Maybe she would after all this was over.

"I considered going to visit my parents for a few days," she said, returning to the original topic. "But Ian knows they live in Erie. And I don't want to drag them into this mess."

"I have an old friend on the force up there. Give me your parents' address and I'll see if he can't arrange for the occasional patrol past their place." Mike put his headset on and stepped back. "Now, shoot a few more rounds, Annie."

She slipped on her earmuffs and returned the target to the end of the alley. She could do this.

Annie studied herself in the mirror. The blonde wig and pale foundation weren't enough to change her appearance or fool a sharp-eyed observer. Sunglasses might bridge the gap, but she needed her disguise to be foolproof. It was time to put her newly found confidence to work.

Ric had installed a new lock on her apartment door when he'd brought her home, but he hadn't stayed long. Still, Annie suspected he was maintaining surveillance from the street. But he couldn't cover all the exits, and the back alley was a shortcut to a nearby second-hand store where she could buy used clothing.

It was time to turn the tables, go hunting, and to visit as many of Ian's old haunts as possible. If anyone could track him down, it was she.

The man outside tossing a bag into the garbage bin looked familiar, but Annie couldn't place him. There were lots of residents in the building she hadn't met. She'd probably passed him in the hallway or shared the elevator with him. He spared her a sideways glance and a nod and nothing more. He didn't seem to recognize her, either.

Nothing unusual happened on the stroll to the shop, but Annie didn't allow herself to relax. If Ian had hired Lucky, he might have another accomplice in place. Her revolver tucked into the small of her back and covered by the oversize blouse was cold against her skin and reassured her she was ready for anything.

Annie had exchanged pleasantries with the elderly female clerk at the store on several trips, The lady involved in her normal game of solitaire, studied the playing cards and barely gave Annie a glance. The store smelled like old people, and the racks held a colorful selection in styles Annie's deceased grandmother had worn. Nothing she'd ever choose for herself, which made them perfect for the occasion.

The bell over the door rang, and from the far corner, Annie peered around a stack of brightly colored flowered blouses to check out the newcomer. At first glance, he looked like the man by the garbage can, but his silhouette reminded her of someone else. She ducked behind the rack. What the hell was Mike doing here?

She had two options. Three, when she thought about it. Slip out the rear door. Hide until Mike gave up, deciding she wasn't there, and left. Confront him.

She slithered through the clothing racks until she was back-to-back with him as he held up a brown suit that appeared to be several sizes too small. "The brown isn't bad, but it won't hide that Dick Tracy profile, Mr. Edwards," she said, pretending to browse through a rack of polyester pants with elastic waistbands.

"And you need to change your perfume, Ms. McGregor," he replied.

She hadn't thought of that. "That's an easy fix."

"What are you up to? You're supposed to be home, behind a locked door, reading a book or watching TV or something." Mike returned the suit to the rack.

"I'm becoming the predator, not the victim. I'm choosing my new wardrobe."

Mike eyed the paisley green and purple muumuu she had slung over her shoulder. "In that?"

"Ian won't look twice at an old lady," she explained, "although this won't give me easy access to my weapon."

"You need a gray wig."

"I was hoping to find one here."

"You shouldn't buy all the pieces of your wardrobe at the same location." Mike turned to face her. "I'll introduce you to a few other places tomorrow. But you need to go home now."

"Does Ric know you're second-guessing

his assignment?" Annie abandoned the muumuu on top of the rack of pants but held on to two flowered shirts.

"No, and you won't tell him." Mike added a headscarf to her small pile.

"I promise. I don't want to hurt his fragile male ego."

Mike chuckled. "You're too new in the business to sneak out from under the watch of one of my best men. Hell, I almost let you get away."

"Is that a compliment?"

"Don't let it go to your head. Now, go home and stay there. I'll be behind you on the way, but you won't see me. Good night, Annie." He waved to the clerk and strode out the door.

She paid for her choices and headed back to the apartment. No matter how she tried, she never caught sight of Mike. That took her conceit down a level or two. Still, he hadn't ordered her to give up her quest. That counted for something.

Behind the closed door, Annie and Mike argued about the arrangements for the night's adventures over the monthly financial spreadsheet. Annie was worried about all the unpaid customer accounts and the lack of cash flow. Mike shut that down, saying he had it handled.

The debate about which bar on the wrong side of town to visit was more intense, as well as how they should get there. Mike insisted on going together, while she wanted to arrive alone. They settled on going together, but parking a block away, and entering the bar five minutes apart. If they didn't sit together, they wouldn't be viewed as a couple, making each of them less recognizable.

They met up at a gas station three blocks from her apartment. If it hadn't been for Mike's old beater of a car, it would have taken her longer to identify the scraggly bum hanging by the front door.

Leaning heavily on the cane she'd snagged from a garbage can, she brushed by him to enter the small convenience store. She wondered if he'd notice that she hadn't worn perfume.

He no longer stood guard when she exited the store, clutching a candy bar and a lottery ticket. She hobbled over to his already-running car, where the passenger side door was cracked open, got in and closed it.

"I still don't like this," Mike said. "But I suppose I can't talk you out of it."

Annie adjusted the gray wig she'd bought earlier in the day. The pixie cut didn't suit her face, but it was another way to throw Ian off. "No. I'm tired of waiting for him to make a move.

The best defense is a good offense, right?"

Mike put the car into gear. "I've never been to this bar. The Coiler, you said? Near the Mexican War streets?"

"If it's still in business. The Health Department should have shut it down long ago."

They didn't talk during the drive. Annie feared that no matter what she said, Mike would twist it into a reason to abort the trip. She guessed Mike was struggling with his protective instincts and the desire to keep her safe versus the need to eliminate the threat Ian represented.

A blinking neon 'OPEN' sign with the P not lit assured the pair that The Coiler was still in business. Mike pulled over a block away and let Annie out. She limped her way to the bar. Thanks to the several pieces of cardboard in her right shoe, she didn't have to worry about losing track of which leg to limp with.

She juggled her cane and tugged the door open. The loud chatter of voices stopped for a moment, then rose again when the patrons determined the new arrival wasn't a threat. Or anyone of interest.

She stopped at the counter and waited for the bartender, a bald man with a well-developed beer belly, to pay attention to her. It took several minutes before he stopped talking to three men at the other end and turned to Annie.

"Whatcha want, Grannie?"

Annie had debated what to drink to

match her disguise. "Can you make a Long Island Ice Tea?" she asked, inserting a quaver into her voice and anticipating the answer. She took the Granny nickname as a compliment to her disguise.

The bartender shook his head. "Not a chance. Pick something else."

"Hmph. You have Iron City, right?"

"Right." He grabbed a chipped mug from the rack and stuck it under the tap.

Annie opened her well-worn clutch purse and dug through it, thumbing through a small wad of bills. Ones, mostly. A handful of change rattled around in the bottom. When the bartender set the beer in front of her, she took a single one out of her purse and laid it on the counter, smoothing it out. Then she took a second bill out and repeated the process. She could practically hear his hopes for a tip slipping away. She dug a quarter out and added it to the stack.

But she wasn't finished with her torture. She took another one and cocked her head, then laid it down, then added a fourth before picking up the beer and taking a sip. Anything more would be out of character. If she needed help, she might have earned some limited sympathy from the bartender.

Beer in hand, she surveyed the small room. Only one other woman was there, and no Ian in sight. She hadn't really expected him. She hobbled over to a small table and sat. If everything went according to plan, Mike would make an entrance soon. He'd be doing the heavy lifting.

Chapter Fourteen

Annie didn't follow either team, but pretended to pay attention to the baseball game on the TV behind the bar. The blurry screen and spirals of cigarette smoke obscured the action. It didn't seem to matter to anyone, and she couldn't let it bother her. The beer soothed her throat enough to keep her from coughing.

The door opened and a small waft of fresh air reached Annie, but she didn't look up. She'd recognize Mike by his voice.

"A Boilmaker," the newcomer said.

Annie studied the reactions of the other patrons. Other than short-lived curiosity, there were none. Perfect. She spared a glance in his direction. He'd added a faded Steelers t-shirt over the plain white tee he'd started with.

As she waited for him to do his magic, Annie noticed a cockroach scuttle across the floor and crawl over the top of her right shoe. She kicked it off and squished it, knowing another would replace it. She wouldn't get rid of Ian as easily.

From the corner of her eye, she saw Mike slip something across the bar to the bartender. Was it money or a picture of Ian? Cash was the grease that allowed for the exchange of information.

The bartender shook his head and turned away to talk to another customer. Mike had been dismissed. Strike one.

With perfect form, Mike tipped his head and poured the shot down his throat, followed by a deep gulp of the beer. If he had too many of those, the night would be cut short.

Annie eyed her own beer and decided she'd be satisfied with half of it. If needed, she would drive Mike home. But he didn't seem to be in a hurry to leave, which hadn't been the plan. He was supposed to leave while Annie waited to see if the bartender placed any calls.

She forced her attention back to the TV screen, but in her peripheral vision, caught the other woman standing, stretching, and ruffling her dyed blonde hair. Amused, Annie watched as the woman unbuttoned one more button of her faded red shirt, and saunter up to the bar to slide onto the stool next to Mike.

She was rough around the edges, with an uneven haircut and nicotine-stained teeth, but not bad looking. Annie hid her grin, wondering how Mike would handle being hit on.

The lady tapped a package of generic smokes on the bar and pulled one out. "Got a light?" she asked.

Not bad for an opening maneuver. Annie wished she could see her face.

"Sorry, I don't smoke," Mike replied. Polite, but no opening for more engagement.

That didn't stop the woman. She nodded. "Good for you. It's a nasty habit." She dug into her purse and retrieved a matchbook, tearing one out, then running it against the strike plate. It didn't even spark, as far as Annie could see. She dropped it in the ashtray on the counter and pulled out a second match. She repeated the process with no luck.

When she opened the matchbook to try again, Mike took a long pull from his beer before turning to the woman. He took the matchbook from her hand and lit a match. First try. From the TV, a cheer arose as the home team scored. The woman raised the cigarette to her lips and Mike moved the burning match closer. She placed her hand on his to guide the flame close enough to light the cancer stick. Annie expected Mike to pull away, but a knot formed in her stomach when he leaned forward and whispered in the lady's ear.

It was like a scene from an old film noir. Mike laid his other hand on his companion's arm, Annie wondered if he had fallen for the woman's dubious charms. But then he pulled away, drained his beer, stood, and walked out the door. He left behind a wad of green paper. The lady snatched it up and tucked it into her bosom before returning to her previous seat.

"Shot down again," she said, eliciting chuckles from her companions.

That was a smooth move by both Mike

and the lady. Annie wondered what Mike had set up.

But it was her turn again. Her job was to track the bartender and see if he made a phone call, perhaps to Ian.

Instead, he wandered over to her table. "You want another one?"

Annie looked down at her empty mug. When had that happened? "I'd better not."

"You know him?" The bartender asked, hovering over her.

Shit. She'd been caught watching. "Who? The man who was here a few minutes ago?"

Annie wiped her eyes with her sleeve and sniffed. Her voice quavered as she answered. "He reminded me of my son. He died a few years back. You would have liked him. Everyone did. Not like this guy. He looked lonely. I rooted for the young lady to pick him up and keep him company."

With a shake of his head, the bartender said, "He was hiding something. Not someone to trust. Are you going to be safe going home?"

"It's not far. I'll be fine." She reached for her cane and stood, leaning heavily on the table. It creaked under the pressure. "Good night."

Once outside, Annie didn't relax. She had to keep to her disguise because of the small cluster of men a few doors down outside another bar. Luckily, Mike's car was parked in the opposite direction. Unfortunately, she had to navigate through a maze of out-of-order streetlights to get there. If she squinted, she could spot Mike waiting.

She started the trek, keeping her eyes peeled for any hazards of the human variety lurking in the shadows. With her cane held firmly in her left hand, she'd be able to grab her gun from her waistband with her right. She paused and stepped into the doorway of a closed dry cleaners shop when a slight shadow separated from the darkness and slithered towards Mike.

Her revolver was in her hand before she even thought about it. She had to get closer. In a crouch, she crept to the next doorway.

The shadow moved through a puddle of light, and Annie hesitated. For a moment, the shadow had seemed familiar.

Mike turned and extended his hand. Annie allowed her right arm to relax, but kept the gun by her side, unsure of what was happening. The overhead car light allowed her to see who the new arrival was. Owen. Coulson's secret weapon. What happened to Owen being her partner?

Or being trusted. She'd been betrayed again.

She shrunk into the doorway, not wanting the two men to see her. She had no one on her side. But for the moment, she had to play the game. At least until Ian was no longer a threat.

Mike and Owen talked for only a minute before they shook hands and Owen walked away and disappeared into the shadows. Annie took a moment to tamp down her emotions and pretend to be unperturbed by the events. She'd make it through this night and rethink her tactics in the morning.

If Mike expected nothing more than a mousy bookkeeper, that's what he'd get. Annie dressed in a long, flowing black skirt and a simple white blouse, and tucked her hair into a bun. Not a trace of an adventurous woman ready to dig through a garbage can or follow a cheater. Plus, it had been one of Ian's favorite outfits, and if he was watching her, he'd be drawn in like a shark to chum in bloody waters.

But she was no victim. No longer. Her revolver was nestled in its holster, strapped to her ankle. A new-to-her derringer rested in her handbag. She'd called the office and told Betty she'd be late, with the excuse of having a migraine. What she'd really done was put in an application at the medical clinic where she'd gone while recovering, then made a stop at a gun store.

Annie thought she'd timed her arrival at the office when it'd be nearly empty, making her an easier target for Ian, but two out-of-town cop cars sat in the parking lot next to Mike's. He'd probably invited some of his friends from his time on the force over for target practice. That ruined her chances of sighting in the derringer on the sly.

"Feeling better?" Betty asked when Annie walked into the office.

Annie continued the charade. "I was worried about being alone. If nothing else, I can fake working on the books. Mike has company downstairs?"

Betty tipped her head towards his office. "No. I didn't recognize his visitors. I was told to make sure they weren't disturbed."

It sounded like something Annie wanted to know about, but she had to continue in the role of a mild-mannered accountant. "No computer access for me, then. I might as well go home."

"I told Mike he should buy you your own. That would free up his office." Betty shrugged. "He said he'd consider it, but that was before this mess with your ex-husband."

The intercom on Betty's desk buzzed. She raised an eyebrow. "How does he do that? He always seems to know when I mention him." She pushed the button to open communication and winked at Annie.

"Yes, Mr. Edwards?"

"Please send Ms. McGregor in."

"Right away, sir."

Annie heard the distinctive click as Mike ended his side of the connection. "Is he tracking me, too?"

"It's all of us, really. When he's here, he doesn't have to ask which of the guys are in the office. I've accused him of having a hidden camera watching the parking lot, but I'm just kidding. He doesn't." Betty tilted her head. "Promise you'll tell me who his visitors are. He didn't introduce them."

Annie paused outside Mike's office to straighten her blouse and skirt. She raised her fist to knock, but Mike called, "Come in."

She opened the door slowly to avoid hitting either of the guest chairs. "Hello."

All three men rose. Mike indicated his chair. "Have a seat, Ms. McGregor. These gentlemen are from McKeesport and would like a word with you."

That couldn't be anything but trouble. Annie hadn't been there for years, but nothing good came from that town. She sized up the men as she walked behind Mike's desk and stood next to his chair. "Detectives," she said before sitting.

"I'm Detective Corey," said the bald one. "And this is Detective Leigh. Please have a seat. We're here to ask you a few questions about your ex-husband. We understand you had a run-in with him recently."

Annie instinctively rubbed her cheek. The

bruise had faded, but not the memory. "You could say that. Unfortunately, he slipped away in the aftermath, and we haven't been able to locate him."

Corey nodded. "We can help you with that. He is in custody in our jurisdiction and suggested you can provide him with an alibi."

Fat chance of that if she could avoid it. "He's mistaken if he thinks I'll help him," she said, shoving back all the resentment she hadn't gotten over, "but I'll tell the truth."

"McGregor is claiming he visited your current residence two days ago. But witnesses place him at the scene of a burglary at that same time."

"There was a break-in at my place, but I don't have any proof it was Ian. I have my suspicions, but that's it. Whomever broke in left by the time I got home. Very little was taken."

Corey consulted his little notepad. "He claims he took clothing, personal items, and a phone. He says he was there for thirty to forty-five minutes around five, but you didn't come home on time, so he left."

"That sounds like what you and Denny found," Mike said. "And the time frame makes sense."

Annie hated helping Ian. "We didn't determine when he was there. The fact that he took the phone seems oddly specific, like the whole thing was a setup. What does he want, to embarrass me? Make it seem like I'm working with a criminal and interfere with my job? What would he want with a cheap blue phone?"

Corey flipped a page in his notebook. "Blue? Like robin egg blue?"

"No, deep blue. The store didn't have much to choose from."

Leigh crunched his eyebrows. "If I remember correctly, McGregor said the phone was white. Why the discrepancy?"

"We used to have a white phone," Annie said. "Ian had this thing where he thought phones had to be black or white. Any other color was unacceptable."

"Because Ian didn't break in." Mike took a step towards his desk. "He called in a favor from a friend. Perfect setup to use as revenge against Ms. McGregor. If it was the man she shot, something was off in his timing or he went outside the parameters of the operation, and didn't have time to get the right information back to McGregor. Until he's fit to be questioned, we won't have the answer."

"It also explains why the lock on my door wasn't damaged. Ian doesn't know how to pick locks," Annie said. "Unless he learned while in prison."

"He claims your door was unlocked and went in to wait. All he wanted was a friendly visit. He took your items as a practical joke." One side of Corey's mouth rose. "Cool story. Admit to one crime to cover another.”

Chapter Fifteen

Annie couldn't catch her breath in Mike's overcrowded office. Mike and the two cops from McKeesport weren't the problem; the unwelcome intrusion of Ian into her life was what sucked all the air from her lungs.

"The DA won't waste time prosecuting such a trivial matter," Mike said. "That's why we decided to not report the break-in."

Leigh leaned back in his chair. "He messed up and obviously underestimated Ms. McGregor. Instead, he's given us all the ammo we need to hold him for an extended period and give Ms. McGregor breathing room. If we convince the prosecutors to request a large bail amount, it's possible to hold him even longer."

"There's also a warrant out for him based on the incident from two weeks ago." Mike crossed his arms. "It may be an option for the City of Pittsburgh to house him."

"We'll see what works out." Corey stood and held out his hand. "Thank you for your cooperation, Ms. McGregor. I assume we can call if you need to testify?"

"Of course. It won't be the first time I've faced him down in court," Annie said.

While Mike showed them out, Annie headed downstairs to the shooting range. Even if

Ian was temporarily out of business, she wasn't ready to let her guard down. In fact, the respite gave her time to strengthen her defenses. She could zero in the derringer while Mike was busy with the cops.

It only held two rounds, and the frequent reloading slowed the process, but she'd only be using it at close range. It wasn't powerful enough to kill anyone unless the bullets were precisely placed. Annie knew which parts of the human body qualified, but hoped she'd never have to use that information.

While studying the shot pattern on the target, she heard the door to the firing range squeak open. Annie leaned back to see the newcomer. Mike, of course.

"What are you doing, Annie?" His voice had a sharp edge.

"What do you mean?" Annie turned to face him.

"The outfit? The new gun?"

She shrugged. "Ian's favorite. Covers me up so other men wouldn't look at me. I hoped to draw him into the open."

"And the derringer?"

"You're a fine example and always carry at least two weapons. Although I don't imagine I'll need it when I get another job. Are there bookkeeping positions that require you to be armed?" Annie absentmindedly stroked the smooth metal handle of the gun.

He put a hand on each of the half-walls that enclosed the shooting station, effectively locking Annie in. "Am I that bad to work for? Or are you letting your ex scare you off?"

"How many of the patrons in the bar last night were stationed there by you? The lady who accosted you was suspicious. Owen was outside. Who else was there?"

"Nobody. And I didn't know Owen was going to be there. He was on a job for Coulson, and our paths intersected. It sounds fishy, and I wondered if Coulson was checking us out, but Owen swears it was coincidence." Mike dropped his arms to his sides.

"And the blonde?" Annie asked.

"Exactly what she seemed. A desperate woman hoping for some extra cash."

"How much did you give her, Mike? Will you account for it as a business expense? Is that why there are so many miscellaneous expenditures with no receipts? How many people's drug addictions are you supporting?"

"The money comes out of my pocket," he said clenching and unclenching his fists. "I never know if it goes in their stomach or their veins. I can't save everyone."

"Are you trying to save me?"

"No. Yes, God damn it," Mike said harshly. "You were. Then you weren't. Now you are again. And I can't make you make sense."

"Stop trying to put me in a box. Even I

don't have me figured out. I've been recreating myself ever since I left Ian." Annie ran a hand through her hair.

"Is that why you're leaving? To change yourself into what? Someone who works a little nine-to-five job, lives in a ratty apartment and has a horde of cats? That's not the Annie I know."

"I want to be trusted. Be successful." She blinked away the threatening tears. "As much as this job has been interesting, I don't have either of those here. I don't fit in."

"Aren't you the person who brought down a ring of thieves? The rest of the guys are envious you pulled that off. More satisfying than catching a cheater, after all."

Annie tilted her head. "And you, Mike? Are you jealous?"

"Of the way you manipulate numbers and a computer? Absolutely. You're the future, and if I'm going to make this agency work, I need you."

It was both a compliment and a dig in a few words. No mention of her usefulness as a PI. Still, Annie would take what she could get.

"You can step into places I can't," Mike continued. "And I normally wouldn't ask this because it's none of my business, but are you religious?"

She'd left her childhood faith when a church counselor suggested she was responsible for the abuse Ian heaped on her. "Not really," she answered nonchalantly, hiding the turmoil inside. "I use the term agnostic."

"Because seeing you in that outfit gave me an idea. I was going to assign it to Jorge, but he's such a ladies' man, I had my doubts." Mike shook his head.

"What does my outfit have to do with it?" Annie asked.

Annie rolled down the passenger side window to get a better look at the old house Mike had parked in front of. She'd lost track of which suburb they were in, but assumed he would tell her when he was ready. Curious, she watched a pair of women dressed in long black skirts, white blouses, and black sweaters enter the home. The shorter woman wore a small black scarf, the other, a white one.

"This is the headquarters of The Sisters of Poverty," Mike explained. "An informal group of ex-Roman Catholic nuns. A trio of women who had issues with the rules imposed by a patriarchal—their words—religious leadership formed a non-profit to serve the homeless population of Pittsburgh. The membership varies, but nuns from other orders support their mission in an informal arrangement."

"What does that have to do with us?" Annie asked.

"Their structure is an echo of the motherhouses they came from. The group is all female, although they allow married women to take part in their activities. One big difference is that they elect their leadership yearly, with no interference from the Roman Catholic Church."

"You've got me interested, Mike."

He grinned. "I went to high school with their current Mother Superior, Sister Hilary Marie. Only I knew her as Patti Jenkins."

"And?" she prompted.

"We bumped into each other a few months back when I was on a stakeout at a grocery store. Since then, we've traded info a few times. Last week she called, looking for help. The sisters are being targeted by a group of young men when they go on missions. It started with name-calling and sexual insults, but last week the canned goods they were taking to a food pantry were snatched."

"That makes no sense," Annie sputtered.

"That's the problem. The question is, who's behind the attacks?"

She began to see the picture. "So you want me to hang out with the sisters and see what I can find out."

"Actually, I want you to act as a bodyguard. They already go out in pairs, but adding a third person shouldn't make a difference to the casual observer. And the sisters will be more comfortable with another woman instead of a man." Mike glanced her way. "You already have the needed outfit. Well, most of it. I'm sure Mother Hilary can find you a headscarf."

"Mother Hilary?"

"That's her title. I haven't floated the idea to her yet." Mike opened his car door. "That's why we're here."

Mother Hilary's office was on the second floor, in what had been a small bedroom in the old house. It was decorated with a variety of motivational posters and a myriad of sticky notes and business cards. Annie tried, but couldn't spot Mike's among them.

Physically, Mother Hilary was diminutive in stature, but had a personality that filled the room. Her black hair was in a bun neatly tucked under a simple white scarf. Her white blouse and black skirt echoed what Annie wore. A bright smile lit her entire face.

"You said you would try to get me some help, but I expected one of your men, not a recruit," she said, folding her hands serenely on her desk.

"Ms. McGregor is my newest employee," Mike explained. "But I realized how perfect she is for this situation."

Like a librarian, Mother Hilary looked

over the top of her rectangular eyeglasses.
"Business must be doing good, if you can afford
to hire a second secretary."

"Not a secretary. I hired Annie as a
temporary bookkeeper to convert my records to
use on a computer." Mike rolled his eyes. "Which
she did, but I still can't figure out how to make
things work, so I've kept her around. Then I
figured out how useful a woman PI could be, so I
added that to her duties and hired her
permanently."

Mother Hilary laughed. "You? Don't you
believe women shouldn't become cops and
belonged at home raising children?"

Mike swiped a hand over the top of his
head. "Yeah, yeah. Life has taught me a few
lessons."

"As it will. Anyway, what do you have in
mind? What can Ms. McGregor do our police
won't? It's not worth their time to chase after a
couple of hooligans."

"She'll join your sisters when they go to
the areas where they have been previously
attacked. With a little luck, the addition of an
extra person will solve the issue."

"I doubt that," Mother Hilary muttered.

"Me, too. But if worse comes to worst,
Annie carries a weapon."

"Where does she hide a gun in that outfit?"

Annie was gripped by a desire to impress
Mother Hilary. She stood, put her foot up on the

chair, and lifted the hem of her skirt. "One," she said. Then she opened her purse and pulled out the derringer. "Two," she continued. "And if needed, I can wear a shoulder harness and cover it with a black sweater." She'd have to buy another gun for that, but she'd eyed a little blue Beretta while at the gun store.

"From a mild-mannered accountant to a walking weapon? That's quite a transformation." Mother Hilary clasped her hands together and rested her chin on them. "I don't know if the good Lord would approve, but I do. Mike, if Ms. McGregor can lead us to a miracle, we'll take a chance on her."

The bus routes the sisters used didn't go anywhere near the distribution spot for their weekly food giveaway, so they carted everything in little red wagons. Sisters Joanna and Marie Bernice chatted cheerfully with old ladies sitting on front steps as they passed by, but Annie noted the tension in their strides. Their steps slowed as the buildings that lined the street became more dilapidated, with boarded-up windows and peeling paint.

For good reason. There were no more friendly neighbors waving as the sisters walked by, and the few people they passed kept their eyes on the sidewalk. Annie would have preferred to walk in front of the sisters, but they knew the route and she didn't, so she stayed a few paces behind and attempted to appear menacing. This excursion had her on edge. She wished one of the guys could have come along as backup, but they would be noticed.

"There they are," Sister Joanna said over her shoulder as two men came into view.

Annie closed the gap and stepped in between the sisters. "Do you want me to do the talking?"

"These are our people. Let us try again." Sister Marie Bernice straightened her spine. "Although I'm not sure these guys are from around here."

Annie gave them points for bravery. Or perhaps foolishness. She wondered if they would credit their faith.

"Hey, looky who's here," the older teen with a shaved head yelled. "Whatcha bring us?"

Sister Joanna slowed her pace and adjusted her hold on the handle of the wagon. The rubber soles on her flat-heeled black shoes made next to no sound as they hit the pavement. "You know where the distribution point is."

"Ha. Like we'd stand in line with all those losers." The bald-headed man sneered. "Besides, I didn't mean your crappy food. I mean the fresh meat you brought."

Annie pretended she didn't realize he was

referring to her and forced herself to stay calm. Still, her hand slipped closer to where her revolver was secured on her hip.

His buddy, who was so skinny he looked as if he'd disappear if he turned sideways, barked out a harsh laugh. "Where have they been keeping you, newbie? On your knees praying in a convent? I can teach you something else you can do on your knees!"

They played rough. Annie faked a yawn, showing her disdain for the tactic. She'd heard worse. "That's all you've got?" she said, deepening her voice.

Baldy said, "Oh yeah? Well, you're so damn ugly that it's illegal for you to be seen in public. That's why you had to become a nun. What's your name, anyway?"

Mother Hilary had suggested an appropriate moniker. "Justice."

"Justice? What kind of crazy name is that?"

Annie pushed her sweater aside, revealing the glint of her weapon. "When justice is done, it brings joy to the righteous but terror to evildoers. Proverbs 21:15."

"Shiiit, I didn't sign up for this," the skinny man said. "This ain't fun no more. I'm out."

"Giving up so soon?" Annie asked. "I was starting to have fun."

"I'm not done yet." Baldy crossed his arms. "I don't believe for a second that's anything more than a fancy toy to you."

She couldn't prove her limited skills without endangering innocent bystanders. Although among the small crowd watching the show, none looked innocent. She patted her gun's handle and grinned. "Are you volunteering to be my target?"

"Hell, no. I'm challenging you to an old-fashioned showdown. Like in cowboy movies."

"You can't do that," Sister Joanna hissed.

Annie ignored her. "When I win," she called, "Do you promise to leave the sisters alone?"

Baldy jerked, as if he hadn't expected her answer. "Not happening."

"Then I'm not sure what the stakes are. Are you ready to make it life or death?" Baldy would have to either step up or back down.

"Every choice has a result, or consequence. Choose wisely. Proverbs 23:7." It was a scrap of a quote she remembered from a Sunday School class years ago.

"The bitch ain't playin'. Give it up," the skinny guy urged.

"Besides, any Saturday Night Special you get won't be a match for my weapon," Annie pointed out. "Your words are shooting blanks."

Baldy and Annie stared at each other. She recognized he wouldn't back down and lose face, but neither would she.

Amid a rustling of fabric, Sister Marie Bernice stepped in front of Annie. "Justice comes in many forms," she said. "What do you see as a fair way to end this, sir?"

"Holy Mary, Mother of God," Sister Joanna prayed in a whisper.

"They got balls. Leave 'em alone," the skinny man blurted out.

"This is our turf." Baldy opened up his arms. "They don't belong here."

"We're just passing through," Sister Mary Bernice fingered the big wooden cross hanging from her neck. "We don't want to mess with your territory."

Not far off, a police siren wailed. The skinny guy yanked on his buddy's sleeve. "We gotta go."

Baldy jerked away. "This ain't over 'till I say it's over."

Annie wished she had backup. She was an accountant with no training in how gangs worked. She didn't have the tools for the job. What had Mike been thinking?

"May we go?" Sister Mary Bernice asked.

"Hell, no." Baldy reached towards the small of his back.

Chapter Sixteen

In the distance, horns blared, the beginning of the lunchtime traffic jam. Close by, a dog barked, setting off a chorus of howls. A flock of pigeons scattered from nearby electric wires. Sister Joanna's prayers had gone silent. Annie ignored all of it as Baldy's right hand disappeared behind his back.

She had a split second to decide if he had a gun, and only enough time to save one sister. Which would Baldy aim at?

Sunlight glinted off the tip of Baldy's pistol as Annie lunged forward, knocking Sister Marie Bernice to the ground. The blast of his gun reverberated among the brick buildings.

When she half-rose to pull her weapon, a second shot knocked Annie backwards. She fought the pain in her left arm. The lessons her shooting instructor had drilled into her ensured she kept a clasp on the handle of her revolver. From her knees, unsure of her aim, she returned fire.

The shell casing rattled to the pavement. Baldy didn't budge and raised his arm for another shot. She took a breath and, with more confidence, she squeezed the trigger a second time.

"Holy Mary!" Sister Joanna screamed.

Baldy dropped to the ground, a red flower blooming on his chest. Annie allowed her right arm to drop before collapsing to a seat on the ground. "Somebody, call the cops."

"You got lucky," the emergency room nurse—Tanisha, according to her name tag—said. She swiped Annie's arm with an alcohol pad, cleaning off the site of the stitched-up bullet wound on Annie's upper arm. "Doctor Braun said the injury, although deep, didn't hit any major arteries, so your blood loss wasn't life-threatening. We'll monitor you for a while, but you shouldn't have to spend the night here. As long as you have someone to take care of you for a few days, that is."

Sammy, the assisting student, giggled. "At last count, there were two cops, one imposing nun, and a handsome older man, arguing over where Ms. McGregor will go when she is released."

Annie wished for one more—the firm's lawyer. The cops would have first crack at her, and she'd need all the legal advice she could get. She'd overheard the staff discussing that Baldy, although severely injured, would survive. At least she wouldn't be charged with manslaughter.

Both Sisters Joanna and Mary Bernice were unharmed. Sister Mary Bernice had skinned knees and palms from when Annie had pushed her down, but hadn't needed anything more than soap and water to clean the scrapes. Sister Joanne was shaken, but physically unhurt.

"We'll keep them away from you as long as possible." Tanisha pushed up the sleeve of the hospital gown Annie wore to examine her work. "But if the cops get a warrant, we won't be able to cover for you for long."

"I don't want you to get into any trouble," Annie said, trying not to flinch as Tanisha slipped a sling over her head. That relegated her to one-handed typing for an undetermined length of time. Even one day was too long. Would Mike fire her?

After the nurse and student left, Annie lay back on the sparse pillow, found a comfortable position for her head, and tried to take a nap, despite the pulsing pain in her arm.

Annie didn't believe in ghosts, but she believed every ghost story she'd ever heard about the Allegheny County Jail after spending an hour in the intake area. At least it was brightly lit, chasing away the spirits. The comings and goings of the odd collection of other arrested men and women kept her distracted from the gloomy backdrop of the old stone building.

Nothing could shield her from curious stares of both the staff and those in custody. She didn't fit in with the assortment of drunks, druggies, and gang members.

The two cops had fought over the need to cuff her on the trip between the hospital and jail. They couldn't put her hands behind her back, according to the doctor's orders, and settled for clipping one side of a cuff to her right wrist and the other to a belt loop. That was more for show than anything else, but Annie wouldn't rock the boat and try to escape.

Mike had explained the whole booking process to her before the cops hauled her away, so she sat quietly, waiting her turn to learn the charges against her and a bond hearing, and dealing with the slowly rising pain. The meds from the hospital were wearing off, and she wouldn't be receiving any more for the foreseeable future.

The screamers worsened her misery—drunks who didn't know where they were or what was happening and druggies on bad trips. The one who thought the world was ending. There wasn't anything staff could or wanted to do for them beyond shoving them into holding cells that did nothing to muffle the screeching. Annie wondered if the ghosts avoided the cells or preferred them for easy prey.

She didn't look around at a bustle of voices at the main desk. Just another prisoner being brought in, she assumed. But at the mention of her name, she glanced up to see a uniformed officer headed her direction, trailed by two other men. He was no street-level cop; and she wondered who he was.

He stopped in front of her. "Ms. McGregor," he said, "Will you come with me, please?"

He didn't appear to be someone people said "no" to often. Annie, being on her best behavior, didn't put up an argument. She waited while her leg shackle was unlocked and then rose, not at all gracefully. The uniformed man reached out to steady her.

"Do you need a wheelchair?" he asked.

"The interview room is only a short distance away, Captain," one cop said.

"I'll be okay," Annie insisted. She digested the fact that he was way up in the ranks while she gathered her balance.

"How often do you get shot, Ms. McGregor?" the officer asked with a hint of a smile.

"Once was enough."

Like Moses leading the Israelites through the Dead Sea, Annie followed the man with a military-style haircut, a path magically opening before them. The room, sparsely furnished with a table and a few chairs was quieter. And when Annie sat, no one moved to secure her to the chair.

"Water," the Captain said calmly.

As if by magic, two bottles of water appeared on the table.

The officer nodded. "Thank you. You can leave now."

"Security protocols," the one cop barked.

"I am aware. Thank you. I don't believe Ms McGregor poses a threat. Not if the intake officers did their jobs. Now, leave. And close the door behind you, please."

Was this all an act? Annie wondered why they would go to such great lengths to entrap her. She remembered Mike's advice. Say nothing about the case until a lawyer was present.

The captain pushed a bottle of water towards Annie. "Help yourself. I suspect you haven't had any since your arrival."

She'd had a few sips while being fingerprinted. They hadn't been able to get clean prints of her left hand, but the technician had handled her with care and given her a glass. She picked up the bottle, but was unable to twist the lid one handed. He reached across the table, took the bottle to open it, and handed it back. Why was he softening her up?

"It seems we each have problems, Ms. McGregor," he said. "I'm hoping we can exchange favors to solve them."

"I know what my problem is," she said. "But what are yours, Captain ...?"

"Jenkins. Captain Frederick Jenkins."

Annie blinked. The name rang a bell. "As in Mother Hilary?"

He grinned and nodded. "Yes, she's my little sister, and that's one of my problems."

"And the others?"

"Your boss, Mike Edwards, two lawyers, and a small band of reporters."

Two lawyers? And what did reporters have to do with her? She dug at the corner of the label on the bottle, trying to peel it off.

"You don't talk much, do you, Ms. McGregor? Silence is usually a tool that cops use."

"I have a world of questions, Captain, but it seems best to let you speak." Annie took another sip of water. She hadn't realized how parched her throat was.

He leaned forward. "My sister wants me to release you, and so does your boss. The lawyers want to make sure you aren't railroaded. And the reporters want an exclusive interview with the savior of Oak Street."

"Who would that be?" Annie crunched her brows.

"You. I suspect my sister had a hand in it, but people are claiming that you—Sister Justice—are responsible for destroying a gang terrorizing that neighborhood."

"I can't comment on that without my lawyer present." Annie stopped. "Lawyers?"

"My sister's doing." He rolled his eyes.

"The organization has a lawyer, of course, but there are a few others she can call."

"What does that mean for me?"

"And that's my problem." Captain Jenkins rested his arms on the table and leaned forward. "Do I allow the legal process to plod along its slow path to the inevitable conclusion or do I use my influence to speed things up and get you released immediately?"

Even without a lawyer, Annie understood which would be better for her. "And would that work?"

"I'll see that all charges are dropped based on eyewitness testimony that your actions were self-defense."

There was always a catch. "And in return?"

"You will have no contact with the press. My sister has offered you sanctuary at the home as a hideout for a few days, although I think she has other motives for that. What they are, I can't figure out."

Annie couldn't find any loopholes. There was always a loophole. She needed a lawyer. Or two.

Sister Joanna set a plate of Salisbury steak and mashed potatoes and gravy in front of Annie, then slid into the chair opposite her with her own plate. "It's nothing fancy, but it's better than jail food."

They were in the dining room of the sisters' home. The large room, a combination of the house's dining room and parlor, was painted pale blue and hosted an assortment of small tables, but half of them were unoccupied. Most of the sisters were out, involved in the various charities they supported.

"What would you know about jail food?" Annie asked.

"Not all of us come from religious backgrounds," Sister Joanna explained.

Annie read between the lines. "I'm sorry," she said. "How bad was it?"

Joanna cocked her head. "You got a taste of it. But each day in jail is worse than the previous one. At least I got meals regularly, even if the food sucked. And before you ask, that's not why I joined the group. I saw what they were doing, and decided I wanted to help so other girls like me wouldn't have to choose between going to jail and eating."

An idea sparked. "I didn't know the group worked with runaways," Annie said, working her way around to her real point.

"Officially we don't. It's one of Mother Hilary's many ideas for the future, but we don't have the time and money right now." Joanna stopped with her fork halfway to her mouth and asked, "Why?"

"A case I've been working on. A girl who went missing when she turned eighteen, so not technically a runaway. I'm stuck. What makes it rough is that her mother waited a long time to ask us to hunt for her. I don't even know where to start."

"I can't share any information about our clients."

Annie nodded. "I wouldn't expect you to. I need to go through police records, but I'm not welcome at any of the cop shops right now."

"For good reason," Joanna giggled. "But Mother Hilary knows someone who can do it."

"Not her brother. I don't want the cops to be aware of the issue without knowing if there's a warrant out for her."

"Good thinking. I won't tell her. But one of our volunteer legal aids spends lots of time in the police records area. The cops won't ask her why she's looking."

That would make it easier, Annie thought. "The girl's name is Kathleen Stanwich. She disappeared five years ago, so she wouldn't be a girl anymore."

Joanna tipped her head. "Not a name I recognize and that's a good thing, but a lot of street people use fake names. Let's see what my friend can find out."

It was something. Better than the nothing Annie was accomplishing while a 'guest' at the sisters' home. She'd agreed to stay a week, but was itching to leave after two days. Until the cops stopped trawling the neighborhood and that one persistent reporter grew tired of his vigil, she was stuck. The news of a cute blonde college student who disappeared from her job at a local coffee shop might be enough to distract him.

Chapter Seventeen

The food at the sisters' home had been nutritious but blandly American and Annie craved something spicier. She paced her apartment, worried the drive to the little Chinese restaurant would be too much for her arm. But she hadn't gone grocery shopping and most of the food in her refrigerator had spoiled during her absence. She considered who she could call to give her a ride.

Mike brought her home after he and Mother Hilary had determined no reporters were staked out near the Poverty House or Annie's apartment complex. She grazed on stale soda crackers as she dumped the spoiled milk down the drain and considered walking to the neighborhood bar. Even a greasy burger would be a treat.

A knock on her door sent Annie reaching for her revolver, but it remained in Mike's safekeeping, along with her derringer. Hugging the wall, she slithered her way to the door and peered out the peephole. The unexpected visitor was welcome.

"Coulson," she said, throwing open the door. "What are you doing here?"

He held up a filled paper bag. "I brought groceries. Can I come in?"

She stepped aside. "How did you know?"

"This isn't my first rodeo. I survived something similar a few years ago. I've brought the makings of omelets or I can take you out."

Either sounded good. Getting away from the loneliness of her apartment sounded better. "Are you asking me out on a date?"

Coulson chuckled. "Mike would kill me. No, I'm doing this as a friend. If you want it to be more than that, you have to make the first move."

She wondered if he was as good as his reputation made him out to be and if it would be worth the risk of upsetting the status quo. "Mike probably knows you're here."

"I waved to Jorge on my way in. I'd expect Mike to do this, but he's your boss, not your friend, so I figured I'd do the honors."

"I'm tired of being good. But with my meds, I can't cut loose, either. What do you suggest?" Annie cocked her head.

"Well, with your arm out of commission, the arcade isn't an option." Coulson's eyes twinkled. "But there's a Brazilian steakhouse I've been wanting to try. Care to join me?"

The restaurant closed at ten, but Coulson took the long way home to check on a stakeout. Typical stuff for his agency, a man claiming workman's comp for a neck injury, suspected of faking it. They hadn't caught him in any unorthodox activities yet, but Coulson was convinced it was a matter of time. Annie didn't mind the detour; Coulson kept her entertained with stories of some of his weirder cases, and she didn't want the night to end.

Jorge no longer haunted the front of the apartment building when they returned. She didn't know if he'd found a different vantage point or if Mike had sent him home. Ian was still in custody, so she didn't need a round-the-clock bodyguard.

Still, Coulson swept the apartment to make sure there were no unexpected visitors before allowing Annie to enter. She waited patiently by the front door while he checked her bedroom and the closets.

"All clear," he reported when he returned. "You should be safe for the night, unless you invite me to stay."

He reached out and touched her cheek. "Tell me to go home, Annie."

She understood the offer and was tempted. It had been a long time since she'd shared her bed. He'd be a fine way to break her celibacy streak. But common sense shot that down.

"I had fun tonight, Coulson, but go home. That doesn't mean you can't come back another time."

"You're a smart woman, Annie McGregor." He started to leave but stopped with his hand on the doorknob. "Don't let Mike give you a hard time. He's your boss, not your father."

Was she being punished or was this Mike's way of keeping her away from Coulson, Annie wondered, as she sat across the street from the home of Mike's latest cheating case, the Freidmann's. Well, Jorge's latest case, but Mike was covering for him since Jorge's mother underwent surgery earlier in the day. And Annie was covering for Mike while he took care of other business.

At least that was the story. The house she'd been assigned to watch was so quiet it appeared vacant. Annie could see the dim glow of night lights, but no overhead lights turned on and off, no matter which angle Annie viewed the house from. But by ten pm., it didn't look any different than the surrounding homes. The entire neighborhood went to bed early.

She yawned and fought to keep her eyes open. She hadn't had time to take a nap, busy with catching up on the paperwork that had piled up while she hid out at the Poverty House. Although that had been two weeks ago, she still mostly worked one-handed, slowing down everything.

Headlights flashed at the bottom of the hill. Annie glanced at her watch. One AM. It must be Mike, checking up on her. The only people out at this time of the night were drunks, druggies, cops and other PIs.

She didn't recognize the car that slowed and parked in front of her. She checked that her doors were locked and wished for her guns, still locked up in Mike's safe. But it was clear who stepped out of the car, based on the profile illuminated by the streetlights.

"Any updates?" Mike asked once he slid into the passenger seat.

"Is this a wild goose chase? Or an elaborate practical joke? Nothing is going on. I don't even think anyone is home."

"It's an expensive joke, but the client, Deidra Freidmann, is insistent her husband George is cheating. I wonder if she's experiencing a medical issue that is causing her to suffer from delusions."

"What do you mean?" Annie rotated her shoulders. It had been a long night.

"It could be the beginnings of dementia, or another condition that results in a personality change. There's a list of conditions that can do that, especially in older people.. I've heard about it, but haven't seen it in action."

"Holy cow. So, what do we do about it?"

Mike shook his head. "We do nothing. I

contact the couple's children and see if any of them have noticed anything strange."

Annie covered her mouth and yawned. "Then can I call it a night and get some sleep?"

"How about we stick it out for another hour? The bars are closing, and people will be coming home."

We? Didn't Mike trust her enough to complete another hour of surveillance?

"I figured it would make time go faster if I kept you company," Mike continued. "You can tell me how the Stanwich case is going."

"You would pick that one," Annie groaned. Sister Joanna's connection had drawn a blank. "I've got nothing. It's like Kathleen doesn't exist. Unless you can get me access to FBI or Social Security records, I'm stuck. Her mother's bank records didn't help either. In fact, they make no sense. She must have additional accounts that we didn't find records for."

"Do you plan to make another garbage run?" Mike raised an eyebrow.

"I'm not sure how productive that would be. Do you have any magic connections you can use? Everyone except me has contacts."

"It takes time. The FBI is beyond my reach, and so is Social Security. I might know someone who knows someone at Stanwich's bank. I'll give it a shot." Mike crunched down in his seat as a car drove up the street, but it kept going, and he sat up again.

Annie laughed. "You're too big to hide that way. I suppose if you're alone, you can lean over into the passenger's seat, but with two of us, you're stuck."

"Every little bit helps."

They sank into silence, watching nothing happen. The neighborhood remained so quiet it was creepy. No dogs howled, no cats prowled the porches. Based on the condition of the homes Annie had seen before sunset—worn looking, but clean and maintained—she would have expected at least one elderly cat lady to live there.

Seated next to Mike, the quiet didn't bother her. She didn't understand why.

The arrangements had been made by phone— once Coulson verified Annie's line wasn't tapped. She snapped on a pair of plastic gloves she'd pulled from the bag strapped to her waist, a 'present' from him. It contained a notepad, pen, flashlight, and the smallest camera Annie had ever seen, and made her feel as if she belonged on the team. Mike wasn't aware of the scheduled expedition to the Stanwich home. As far as he knew, Annie planned to spend her rare night off catching up on housework and reading.

"What are you looking for?" Owen

whispered. "Coulson didn't tell me."

Owen and Annie had parked a block from the house. Mrs. Stanwich was at her weekly bingo game, and Annie hoped she'd have a winning night. That way, she'd stay longer.

"If Kathleen's bedroom hasn't been remodeled, I want to search it." She couldn't believe that she was actually doing this. "That and get my hands on Mrs. Stanwich's financials. Where is her money coming from?"

"That's a tall order for a couple of hours. Which is your priority?"

Her heart urged her to visit the girl's room. She wanted to sit in the middle and figure out who Kathleen was. Did she have posters on the walls? What books did she read? Or had her parents wiped out every trace of her existence? Her brain insisted the mother's money situation held the answers she needed. "Bank records, first."

Owen nodded and opened the car door. "Reminder—what we're doing is illegal. This is your last chance to back out."

If they got caught, the rest of Annie's life would be ruined. The cops wanted a reason to put her behind bars. At the same time, she'd destroy every bit of Mike's limited trust. On the upside, she might solve the puzzle of the Stanwichs. "Let's do this," she said, opening her own door.

Owen led the way, Annie trailing behind,

admiring the graceful way he moved. When they reached the home, he unlocked the back door as easily as if he had a key. Enough nightlights illuminated the house for her to see where she was going. They didn't stop in the kitchen but made their way to what appeared to be a study.

It couldn't be that easy. Annie settled on the floor beside a two-drawer wooden file case and pulled a pen flashlight from her back pocket. She tugged on the top drawer, it didn't open. She turned to ask Owen for help but remembered his admonition to remain silent.

He stood across the small room, rifling through the drawer of a full-size metal cabinet. Annie clicked her fingers twice, the agreed-on signal. Owen hurried over, pulled out a short, slender piece of metal, stuck it in the keyhole, and twisted it. This time, when Annie tugged on the drawer, it opened.

In the dim glow of her flashlight, she flipped through the files, until she came across one with birthday cards drawn by a child. On the back, each was marked with a year. If she did the math right, Kathleen would have made them from age three to ten.

Annie wondered why they stopped. Was there another file with additional cards?

Not that she could find. Most of the other cards were a variety of greeting cards from Christmas and other holidays. She wished she had time to browse through them. They might give her insight into Mrs. Stanwich's motivations.

Owen set a slim manila folder on the top of the file cabinet and returned to the other side of the room. Annie switched her attention to the most recent bank statement, but it didn't seem to offer any new information.

A brilliant light shone through the office window and Annie froze as she reached for the second drawer. Damn it, Mrs. Stanwich shouldn't be home so soon. With no time to get the bank file back to Owen, she stuck it under a legal envelope on the desk. With any luck, Mrs. Stanwich would think she'd left it there.

But the light faded away.

"Just a car going around the corner," Owen whispered. He rotated a finger in the air, a signal to get back to work.

The return address label on the envelope caught Annie's eye. Gates, Rodney, & Greeley, it read. One of the biggest law firms in the area. Annie slipped the contents out of the already opened envelope and shone her little light on them. It was better than she had expected. The Last Will and Testament of Herbert Gerald Stanwich.

Reaching into the black bag at her waist, Annie pulled out the small camera. She couldn't take the documents with her, but she'd get pictures of a few of the pages. Between juggling the flashlight and the camera, the results would be less than perfect, but would give her something to work from.

With the task completed, Annie struggled to slide the thick document—Mr. Stanwich had gone into great detail about what he wanted done with his estate—back into the envelope. Owen came to assist her, then tapped his watch and held up his hand, fingers stretched open. Five minutes. Annie didn't think she'd find much else in that amount of time.

She pointed one finger upward. Enough time remained to check out the bedroom situation. Owen nodded.

"I'll clean up here," Owen whispered in her ear.

She gave him a thumbs up before turning and leaving the room. She'd spotted the stairs on the way in and sprinted up them, mindful of the time limitations.

All five doors were open, including the bathroom, and that made her task simple. All she needed to do was poke her head inside. Quick and easy. Identifying Mrs. Stanwich's room was first—the smell of her rose-scented perfume struck Annie's nose as she got close. But that room didn't appear to be the master bedroom, and Annie wondered if she'd changed rooms after the death of her husband.

None of the three other rooms had any personality. They were tastefully decorated in boring shades of wheat and pink. Not one appeared to have been used by a teen-age girl.

Annie wondered what sort of mother would so easily wipe away all traces of her daughter.

Owen waited at the bottom of the steps. Annie shook her head as she came down. She could explain the details once they returned to Coulson's office.

"So, how does it feel being a criminal?" Coulson asked, half an hour later.

Annie blinked. "I hadn't thought of it that way. But the answer is alive. I feel alive. It's addictive, isn't it?"

Owen chuckled.

Coulson nodded. "Hang onto that feeling. And never pull a stunt like that on your own."

Mike would never approve of her doing anything illegal. But she'd done it for Kathleen. "I promise."

They all left. Owen to his home, her and Coulson to an all-night coffee shop. Annie still didn't make the first move.

Chapter Eighteen

The office was empty except for Betty when Annie arrived after a trip to the courthouse. Not an unusual occurrence and it suited Annie fine because she wanted to concentrate on dissecting the paperwork she'd picked up. Herbert Stanwich's will.

She hadn't even bothered getting the pictures developed. The glimpses she'd had at the house convinced her it contained the information she needed. She feared she wouldn't be able to wade through the mounds of legalese.

"When is Mike expected?" she asked Betty.

Betty shook her head. "He hasn't checked in. But he left something on your desk. At least, I'm guessing it was him."

"What is it?"

With a broad smile, Betty said, "Go see."

Annie peeked around the corner. "Holy shit."

"Yeah, that's how I reacted. It's about time."

Computer components were scattered on her desk. A keyboard, monitor, mouse and the computer itself. Not assembled, but that wasn't a surprise. Annie couldn't imagine Mike tackling the chore himself.

So much for plans for a quiet moment. Her plans for the day had just changed. She hoped Mike had bought all the bits and pieces she needed to get it running.

"Did I miss something?" Mike asked. "I thought you'd be glued to the screen."

Annie looked up from her paperwork. She'd assembled the computer, but left it turned off. "You bought everything but an extension cord and floppy disks. I don't have enough electrical outlets."

"What are floppy disks?"

"A way to share files between your computer and this one. You've heard me talk about them."

He rubbed his forehead. "And I didn't understand. But I'm sure you'll show me."

"After you help me with something." Annie handed him several pages of the will. "We aren't working on this case anymore, but I was curious. I've highlighted several parts. Do they mean what I think they means?"

Mike scanned the papers, then pulled a nearby chair to Annie's desk and sat. "Where did you get this?"

"County records. That mystery TV show that's so popular sparked the idea." Annie knew

Mike despised the show, so she waited for his comeback.

Which didn't happen. His eyebrows furrowed as he flipped to another page. "How long until a person is presumed dead?" he asked, without glancing up.

"Seven years is the standard, although courts have the option of changing that depending upon circumstances." She'd looked it up in Mike's collection of law books.

"And how long has Kathleen been gone?"

"Mrs. Stanwich told us five. I did the math, and it's been over six."

"So, her father left her a substantial sum of money. Not enough to make her a millionaire, but enough to make a difference in her life."

Annie nodded. "And if I'm right, Mrs. Stanwich can have her declared dead soon, and the money will revert to her."

"Since Mrs. Stanwich appears to be having money issues, she needs to get her hands on that trust." Mike flipped to the next sheet in the stack. "So, she's covering her bases by pretending to look for her daughter, without putting effort into it."

"Unless we find Kathleen, we can't stop her." Annie picked up a pen and tapped it on her desk.

"We have no proof she's not dead."

"What am I missing? What other records can I check?"

"I had a friend check out driver's license records and he drew a blank. I don't have the connections for neighboring states, but she could be anywhere." Mike shook his head. "If she changed her name, even Social Security records won't help. If you locate any of Kathleen's high school friends, they might be able to provide clues."

"Mrs. Stanwich didn't share any of that information." Annie frowned. "It's like she didn't know anything about her own daughter."

"Have you checked her high school yearbook? The local library might have a copy, or the school itself. There might even be someone there who remembers her."

Annie had been a good student and never needed to visit the principal's office in school. Still, she took extra care when she dressed in a pale blue suit for her appointment with Principal Brett Hartley. She didn't want to look too official or aggressive, hoping to gain Hartley's sympathy.

She earned more than one side-eye from students in the hallway during the short trip to the office. Whose mother did she remind them of?

Principal Hartley met her at the door of his small office. After exchanging pleasantries, he got right to the point. "I was a teacher when

Katy was a student," he said. "Still, I didn't remember much about her until I looked up her records. So, tell me why you're asking? You say she disappeared but didn't give me any details."

"I don't have many," Annie explained. "Her mother hired the firm to find Kathleen, but didn't supply us with the information needed for a comprehensive search. All we know is she left home on the day of her eighteenth birthday, a day or two after she graduated."

"I recall," Hartley said, "That she was a bright student but so shy that it was easy to forget she existed. Group projects were a nightmare for her, and she didn't participate in any extracurricular activities. That limited the number of colleges that would consider her application despite her high marks. If she even went to college. I wondered if she was being abused, but there were no outward signs of it."

"Would the school records show if her transcripts were forwarded anywhere?"

"That's a question for my clerical staff. But tell me again why you want to find her?" Hartley pushed his chair back. "I won't invade a student's privacy without due process."

"Here's the thing. Mrs. Stanwich hired us, then refused to cooperate with the investigation and stopped paying the firm." Annie cocked her head. "In the short time I was officially on the case, I didn't find any leads about Kathleen, either before or after her disappearance. I wondered about the abuse angle but couldn't uncover any proof. But I kept digging, and uncovered information that would benefit her monetarily."

"You said you're not working for her mother anymore?"

"That's correct. I'm not getting paid for my time. And I won't expect payment from Kathleen, either."

Hartley crossed his arms. "Since when do PIs do community service, Mrs. McGregor?"

"It sounds like you've met some of my coworkers, Principal." Annie grinned. "Ruthless bastards to the core, and they'll admit it. But I'm not your standard PI."

"I wouldn't normally do this, but I'll see what I can find. We didn't do enough to help Katy when she was here. I can make it up to her now."

A shiver ran down Annie's spine when Bobby Hansen pulled into a parking spot a block away from The Flats Lounge, in the off-again, on-again case. She had no desire to repeat the events of her earlier visit. Despite having shot two men herself, the horror of finding the dead body of Harold Rimer still haunted her. Without her gun, still locked in the safe in Mike's office, she felt exposed as she slunk into the bar, hoping Bobby wouldn't notice her arrival.

The night's music was what Annie expected. George Strait crooned about Fort Worth, but no one listened. The establishment was packed, so the song couldn't be heard, anyway. She slithered her way through the crowd to the bar and bought her first beer. By the time she turned around, Hansen had vanished into the cigarette-smoke haze.

A wind-driven blast of cold air from the opened front door cleared the air enough for Annie to spot him with a group of men near the back hallway. Annie moved to a spot next to the wall to monitor them without drawing attention to herself. The men laughed loudly, but she was too far away to hear the joke. Sipping her beer, she tried to blend in with the desperate women hoping to find a warm bed and willing companion to spend the night with.

She'd seen most of the men with Hansen before. If not at this bar, maybe at another one she'd followed him to. She wished she had Coulson's miniature camera with her—she'd like to find out if any of her coworkers recognized any of them. The group included the man he'd been with at the Chinese restaurant. None of that meant anything. For all Annie knew, they were nothing more than old friends. Certainly, they dressed alike in polo shirts and khakis. Too upscale for this establishment, and not trying to fit in.

But old friends didn't keep looking over their shoulders. Were they waiting for someone or checking if they were being watched? Annie tried to track them without being caught, but hadn't perfected the art of using peripheral vision.

She caught them passing something among themselves, but didn't recognize the small, rectangular box. Too skinny to hold anything, even drugs. She couldn't mingle with the group and get her hands on one. She needed Owen's skills.

Her beer mug was empty, Annie realized, and she considered calling it a night and heading home. She hadn't learned anything new to report to Mrs. Hansen, and her tolerance for alcohol was low after a month of abstinence. Her stitches had been removed only two days earlier. Pride in her job warred with common sense, and she headed to the bar for a second round.

Her timing was impeccably bad. Half the customers had the same idea, and while she waited for her turn, she listened to the gossip, but she didn't know enough about the high school teams to take part. By the time she got a fresh mug and twirled around, the group Hansen was part of had shrunk. It took her a moment in the dark bar to realize she'd lost him.

One man walked towards the back. There

wasn't a parking lot out the back door, but that's where the restrooms were. Not that Annie would use the women's room—she'd checked it out on her last trip, and it looked as if it hadn't been cleaned in over a year.

But there'd been three doors in the hallway. Annie had assumed the third led to a closet or stockroom. Were Hansen and his buddies in there?

Then Hansen sauntered down the hall, adjusting himself. Annie pretended not to notice. She abandoned her beer on a nearby table and headed home.

"Tell me again how this works," Mike said. "I don't understand how I see the changes you make when you're working on your own computer."

"By using these." Annie held up a box. "These are floppy discs. We can save files on these and we both can use them."

Mike blinked rapidly. "Be patient with me. You'll only have to show me about a hundred times before I get it."

"Betty can be in charge of them. She doesn't have to use them, just keep track of who has them. Like a librarian checking books in and out."

"The salesman showed me how it works, but went so fast I got lost." One side of Mike's mouth rose. "Step by step, take me through the process."

Annie opened the box and took out one. "This is a floppy disk. It's storage. Instead of saving information on your computer, you can save it on this."

She started to insert the disk, but stopped. It stirred a fresh memory, accompanied by an older one. "Holy shit."

Chapter Nineteen

Annie spent the hour waiting for Coulson to arrive by copying files from Mike's computer to floppy discs. Coulson didn't bring Owen along since his part of the operation came later.

"Explain it to me," Coulson demanded. "What's so important about these little pieces of plastic?"

Sitting in front of the computer, while Mike and Coulson sat on the other side of Mike's desk Annie said, "Information. They store information. What can be done with it if it's stolen?"

"I'm beginning to understand," Mike said. "What if Coulson got his hands on my financial information? Or my list of clients?"

"Me? I wouldn't do that," Coulson protested.

"But if the two of you weren't friendly rivals, you could put Mike out of business." Annie tapped a few keys, then pushed a button to pop the disk out of the computer. "In my hand, I hold a list of names, phone numbers, and addresses of Mike's contacts. How much money would I get if I sold this to the highest bidder?"

"But you won't." Mike rubbed his chin. "What if one business bribed the employee of another to pass along the info? It's a new level of industrial espionage."

"Don't big companies have methods to prevent it?" Coulson asked.

"I'm sure they do." Annie fiddled with the floppy disk she held. "One of the biggest changes is how many people are buying computers, so exchanging information is so much easier."

"It's over my head," Mike frowned. "What do you suspect Hansen of stealing? Passing discs around a group doesn't sound like selling confidential information."

"That's why Annie needs to get her hands on one, to see what it says. And that's where Owen comes in," Coulson pointed out.

"Fair warning. Information can be stored in different ways." Annie tipped her head. "My computer may not be able to read what's on the disk, depending on what program was used."

"Whatever that means. I don't understand half of this." Mike shook his head. "I feel like a dinosaur."

"Me, too. I think I'm so smart, but then Annie starts talking and I'm lost. Are you sure I can't steal her from you, Mike?" Coulson grinned.

"I should start my own firm," Annie said with an expressionless face. "Contract out to small companies to provide computer services."

Coulson nodded. "Sign me up. In fact, I'll finance your start-up. For a small share of the profits, of course."

Annie had been joking, but a spark of

excitement flashed in her brain. Own her own business. Was it possible?

She and Owen had become the best of friends. Not really, but they worked to make it appear that way, sitting in the back booth of the Chinese restaurant. This was their first chance to track Hansen. But it didn't appear there'd be a break in the case tonight, as he was sitting alone.

Annie suspected both Mike and Coulson were close by, but hadn't spotted either. She'd argued with Mike about returning her guns—Owen didn't carry—but he'd refused. He claimed he had to clear it with Captain Jenkins first. Plus, he wanted to send her through training again, to correct any issues that might have been caused by her injury. Annie suspected he was worried she might be trigger-happy.

"Do you suppose he got stood up?" Annie asked as she set her chopsticks aside and picked up a fork.

"Or he likes the food here." Owen chuckled. "I can't understand why. A bunch of places have better Chinese. One's a few blocks away. I'll take you there someday."

"I'll take you up on that." Annie twirled her fork in her fried rice, then pushed it aside. At least the honey chicken was decent. "What's he doing now?"

Owen had taken the side of the booth facing Hansen, shielding Annie's face so she wouldn't be recognized. "Nothing interesting. Sipping his tea. Perfectly normal. Rather disappointing, I'd say. That's the way it goes."

"Ain't that the truth."

They continued to pick at their food, while Owen monitored Hansen. "So, what's with you and Coulson?" Owen asked, breaking the silence.

"What do you mean?"

"I told you we'd run interference if you wanted. You're spending lots of time with him, but haven't given us a signal to be extricated."

"He's leaving any moves up to me. I haven't succumbed to his charms yet." It took Annie a minute to process the implications. "Wait. You and the guys are gossiping about me?"

Owen snorted. "Not me. I stay out of it. But them? They're nothing but a bunch of matchmaking biddies. It's bad enough they have a pool going."

"Betting on what? Our first kiss? Or when Coulson talks me into sex?"

"Neither. They're trying to figure out who will get the girl—Coulson or Mike. The theory is that it's about time someone breaks through that icy exterior Mike displays, and they're laying odds on it being you."

She needed to shut down that train of thought immediately. "He's my boss. Nothing's going to happen."

Owen grinned. "We'll see."

Annie stared at the list of dates when Hansen had been followed and done something worth noting in the case file. There was a pattern there somewhere, but she couldn't find any rhyme or reason to his activities. He wasn't cheating, as far as she could prove. She closed the folder and set it on the corner of her desk. Sitting outside his home every evening, waiting to see if he'd leave, was a waste of time.

Hansen wasn't the worst of her worries. Ian had been released from jail and put on probation. Which meant he had a week or more to disappear into the network of his friends and avoid law enforcement, and giving him time to plot his next move against her.

She 'd kept her concerns hidden from Mike. He had enough worries of his own. The past three months, the business had stayed in the red.

Betty stuck her head around the partition. "Why don't you head home, Annie? Nothing is happening here. Jorge called and said he was on his way in, so I won't be alone. I know you worry about that.”

“Where’s Mike?”

“Who knows?” She shrugged. “It’s like the old days when he’d be gone for hours on a case with only me to hold down the fort. But it was a job, and he paid mostly on time.”

What would Betty do if Mike had to shut down the agency? Annie couldn’t save the world. Hell, she couldn’t save even one tiny piece of it. “I have errands I’ve been putting off,” she said. “See you tomorrow.”

Annie pushed open the door to Mike’s office without knocking, waving a paper in the air. “I found her!”

“Good morning to you, too,” Mike said, putting down the file he held, picking up his coffee cup, and taking a deep swallow. “Who, where, and how?”

She pulled a chair up to his desk. “Kathleen Stanwich. Up north, in Edinboro. She made the college’s Dean’s List and is in my alumni newsletter.”

“Luck counts.” Mike grinned. “Do you have an address and phone number?”

“Not yet. At least I know where to start. One of my old friends works there. I haven’t talked to her in forever, but it would be a good time to catch up." Their friendship had been another victim of Ian's abuse.

"When was the last time you visited your folks?"

"I called them a couple of weekends ago." She'd been avoiding them until her arm healed.

"You should go visit them. Make a long weekend of it. In fact, if you include Friday and Monday both, it'll be a mini-vacation."

Annie was no dummy. "You're trying to get me out of town. What have you heard?"

"Ian is out and plotting his next step. Why didn't you tell me, Annie?" Mike swiveled his chair and unlocked his file cabinet. He took her weapons out and placed them on his desk.

"I'm tired of running and hiding. I won't have any peace until I can get him out of my head."

"Are you talking about killing him?" Mike put his hand on top of her revolver. "I can't allow you to have these, if that's the case."

Annie shook her head. "No. I want him dead, but I'll leave his punishments to the legal system. But I'll do whatever I can to give the cops everything they need to make sure he never gets out of jail again."

"You plan to set a trap for him?"

"Are you in? I promise not to do anything that would go against your ethics."

Mike shook his head. "Coulson is rubbing off on you."

How much did Mike know about her relationship with his rival?

He pushed her guns towards her. "Head downstairs. You're going to be rusty. I'll join you in a minute."

"All clear." Jorge's voice squawked through the walkie-talkie on her seat. "Go ahead and get your groceries."

Annie flipped on her turn signal, then picked up the walkie-talkie and pushed the button to talk. "10-4. But I still say this is silly."

After her return from Edinboro—which had been extended to a week but with no contact with Kathleen—Mike insisted on upping Annie's security. He claimed the word on the street was that Ian had hired help to get revenge on her.

"He's got sources we don't." Jorge flashed his headlights in acknowledgment of her change in direction. He was sticking to her tail and making it clear they were traveling together.

Annie made her turn into the grocery store's parking lot before responding. "There's been no sign of Ian anywhere. Hell, he's even stopped calling the office."

She pulled into a parking spot. Jorge followed. "Mike's operating from a gut feeling, he's rarely wrong."

"That's the reason I haven't fought his decision." Annie turned off the truck, undid her seatbelt, and tucked her revolver into the holster on her side, making sure her jacket covered it. "I'm heading in."

She lay the walkie-talkie on the passenger seat, not wanting to haul it around the store. Ian hadn't set foot in a grocery store for most of their marriage, leaving that chore to her. So, nothing bad was going to happen except she might spend too much money on ice cream.

The store was busy but not crowded, and Annie took her time browsing the shelves. It was such a good day that even the normally grouchy cashier smiled at her.

Hidden behind heavy storm clouds, the sun was setting when Annie pushed her cart out of the store. The streetlights flickered on and off and on, hesitant to commit to the changing twilight.

Chilly winds blew a mix of dead leaves and litter across the lot. Other shoppers pushed their carts to their vehicles. Annie had parked towards the end of the lot, hoping no one would block her in. It had worked. Jorge's car was the only one close to her. He flashed his lights. The coast was clear.

She paused to tug her jacket closed and

didn't notice the speeding car until it stopped beside her. Instinctively, she reached for her revolver. She was too slow.

Her head slammed against the pavement.

She couldn't see. Or move. Or yell. There was something in her mouth, stopping her, causing her gag reflex to spark. No light filtered through whatever covered her eyes.

But she could still feel. And hear. Every bump that jostled her, each harsh laugh from the others in what Annie guessed was a car. She listened but heard nothing besides the roars and sputters of other vehicles. No police sirens. No blaring horns. Had Jorge abandoned her?

Neither of the men talking was Ian. She would have recognized his voice. Annie didn't know if that was a good or bad thing.

She wiggled, trying to free her hands. A hard object poked her in the ribs. She groaned.

"At least she's still alive."

"She's better looking than I expected."

"She won't be by the time he's done with her."

The car turned sharply, throwing her against the back of the front seat. Annie used the moment to try to free her arms, with no luck.

The move earned her a harder poke in the ribs. The new road seemed to be an endless path of potholes, and the driver was determined to hit each one harder than the one before.

The car stopped abruptly, the engine turned off, and doors opened. Two sets of footsteps moved away. Annie was alone.

Chapter Twenty

An owl hooted. With the doors of the car open, the night air rushed in. She shivered. With tentative movements, she tried to find a comfortable position, or one that would allow her to get out of the car. If nothing else, perhaps she could rip off whatever covered her eyes.

They'd stripped her of her revolver; no surprise. She felt naked without it. She wouldn't be able to use it, anyway; they'd bound her hands and feet. Her derringer was at the office, locked away. Annie hadn't imagined needing it for a simple grocery run.

Her stomach churned as three voices got louder. She knew the third one too well, and not in a good way.

"Well, well," Ian chuckled. "What do we have here? Take the hood off, boys."

Hands wrapped around her ankles, and she was pulled, belly-down, out of the car, then hauled across the gravel surface. A hard kick to the side, and Annie curled into a fetal position. Ian gravitated towards steel-toed boots.

She clamped her teeth on the fabric that filled her mouth, not wanting to give him the satisfaction of listening to her scream. He liked to see himself as the one in charge, all powerful, in control of her destiny. She'd learned not to feed his delusions.

Annie rolled away from the foot planted in her side. When the fabric that covered her head was pulled off, she blinked, bracing for blinding bright lights. But the place was pitch dark. No streetlights, no nearby homes, nothing. Not even the moon shared its feeble radiance.

Brightness flared, and Annie squeezed her eyes shut.

"You're too pretty for your own good," Ian hissed. "How many men do you have panting after you? You should be punished for that."

What came next was not a slap on the cheek. A hard fist rammed into her nose. The cloth gag protected her from biting through her tongue. Warm liquid streamed down her cheek. Despite her best effort, a trickle of a moan escaped her lips.

"You always did look good in red," Ian chortled. "You should wear more of it."

Annie tensed, anticipating the next blow. Instead, Ian reached down and wiped the blood from her cheek, then rubbed it over her entire face.

"That's better," he said with satisfaction. "Stand up, bitch."

Annie's hands and ankles remained tied, making it impossible. She didn't even try.

He kicked her thigh several times. Not as hard as the first kick, but enough to leave bruises later. If there was a later.

"Pick her up," he ordered.

They grabbed her by her armpits and jerked her upright. Without their help, she'd fall back to the ground.

"Did you search her?" Ian asked.

"Yeah." The man holding her left arm said. "Not that it was any fun, what with her being unconscious. Only found the one piece."

Ian nodded and pulled Annie's gun from his waistband. "A sweet one. A little on the small side, but not bad." He juggled it between his hands. "Never imagined you with a gun." He grasped it firmly in his right hand and swung it, striking her on her cheek.

Her knees collapsed, but she still didn't scream.

"You've gotten tough in your old age." Ian grinned and pointed her gun at her. "But even you can't stop a bullet. Don't worry, I'm not through with you yet."

He raised his leg, and, ninja-style, kicked her in the stomach hard enough that the force of the blow knocked both her and her captors backwards. Her breath left her body. She collapsed and wished for darkness to descend and end the torture.

The shot that was fired sounded too far away to be from her revolver. Or her brain wasn't working right. She waited for the round to slam into her bruised and bloodied body.

Two shots followed and a heavy weight

dropped onto her, once again knocking the oxygen from her lungs.

"Annie," Mike's voice said. "Stay with me, Annie. An ambulance is on its way."

She blinked her eyes. Where had Mike come from? The weight disappeared, and the gag ripped from her mouth.

"Say something, Annie. You're going to be okay."

Through her swollen eyes, Annie couldn't count how many tubes were attached to her arms. She couldn't see much of anything. The medical equipment beeped and hissed, and something sounded like heavy breathing, reassuring her she hadn't died. She wasn't able to turn her head to identify where the breathing came from. There didn't seem to be a reason to stay awake, so she closed her eyes.

When Annie woke again, she wished she hadn't. Everything hurt. Even her eyes. She opened them farther this time, but wasn't able to look around. At least the covers of the florescent lights over her bed displayed a mosaic pattern, giving relief from the endless white.

"Hello there, Annie," Mike said. He stood at the end of her bed where she could see him. "Glad to see you're with us."

"How long have I been out?"

"Two days. The docs kept you sedated to stop you from thrashing around and doing more damage. But they decided there's no internal bleeding, no broken bones, so it was safe to let you regain consciousness. They reset your nose, and after a few weeks, it should be back to normal."

"I thought I was dead, Mike," she said, clutching on the thin blanket that covered her. The beeping of the monitors sped up.

"Are you cold? There's a spare blanket at the end of the bed." He grabbed and unfolded it, then draped it over her. "Is that better?"

She nodded and closed her eyes. Stoic Mike wouldn't acknowledge her concern.

Then his hand ran over the top of her head.

"I know it was bad, Annie. I got there in time to stop it."

She ran her tongue over her lips before asking, "What happened to Ian?"

His hand was removed from her head, and she fluttered her eyes open. "Mike?"

"He's dead. Along with one man who helped him."

She studied his face. "You?"

A shadow of a grin glanced across his face, then vanished. "The cops aren't sure who fired the killing shots. Detective Myers is taking the credit—or blame—for it. The coroner found

three separate entry wounds, but the powers
that be decided not to waste taxpayer money to
determine which one belonged to which gun."

She didn't know how to feel about that.
She didn't know how to feel about anything.
Annie closed her eyes. "Don't leave me."

"You haven't been alone since we got to
you. We've been taking turns sitting with you,
including your parents and the Sisters of Poverty.
I'm going to pass the word along that you woke
up and someone will be here in a minute."

Annie didn't have the energy to stay
awake long enough to find out who her next
visitor would be.

Annie stared at the computer screen. Or past it,
really. She found it hard to concentrate for more
than a few minutes.

She hadn't been alone since her release
from the hospital. Here at the office, one of the
guys always hung around, as well as Betty. When
she ran errands, she was accompanied to the
stores. Once she got home, whoever was on duty
held an overnight vigil, watching her apartment
windows for lights that didn't belong. She'd
started keeping track of who got the assignment.
Mike and Coulson stayed pretty much even.

Not that there was any threat to her. At

least, not that anyone had shared with her. It was Mike's way of fighting the nightmares she'd confessed to. She'd refused his offer to camp out in her living room. Coulson had offered to share her bed and hold her tight all night long and she'd turned that down, too.

No matter how hard she stared at the computer screen, the numbers didn't change, and they weren't good. Mike and the others spent far too much time guarding her instead of working. She needed to quit.

Her phone rang, pulling her out of her contemplation. "Edwards Agency, McGregor speaking." She'd have to think about changing her name.

"Hey, girl, it's Joannie."

Joannie was her friend who worked at Edinboro University. "Hey, I thought you were ignoring me," Joannie said. "You need to get an answering machine. I've tried to call you at home a couple of times."

Annie had unplugged her phone once calls from reporters started rolling in. Another thing to add to her list—change her number.

"Tell me you have good news."

"It is. I heard from Kathleen."

For the first time in weeks, a surge of excitement stirred in Annie's chest. "Did she agree to meet with me?"

"Yep. On the condition she can bring her boyfriend along."

"I don't have a problem with that. How can we coordinate getting together?"

"I expected that question." Joannie said. "She asked that I act as a go-between. I get the impression she's seen some shit and wanted protection in case something goes wrong."

"I don't blame her for that. Ask her about next week." Annie pretended to flip through her desk calendar. "Thursday? Say around eleven? That will give me time to drive up. Then we can have lunch."

"That works for me. I'll call you."

"Call me here. If I'm out of the office, Betty can take a message." Like that would happen. Annie wasn't going anywhere.

Mike wouldn't let her go alone. Or drive the 200 plus miles. He even picked her up in what he jokingly called 'his good car', a screaming yellow 1975 Camaro not built for undercover surveillance. She spent most of the trip staring out the window. Mike wasn't good at small talk, but at least she got to enjoy the scenery.

They'd agreed to meet up near the lake on the west side of town, near the Plum Street bridge. Not in a park, but at a spot where college kids liked to hang out. No one was in sight when she and Mike arrived; classes were in session and the chilly temperatures kept people away. Holding a large manila envelope, Annie zipped up her jacket before getting out of the car. A quick glance didn't reveal anyone waiting, but they'd arrived early.

"Should we wait in the car?" she asked. "Keep the motor and heat going?"

"I have a blanket in the trunk," he said. "If you're cold, you can wrap up in it."

"Not yet." She was trying to prove to herself that she wasn't fragile. She jerked her head towards the small stand of trees along the lake's shore. "They'll block the wind."

They walked the short distance to the grove, Annie carefully placing her feet on the uneven ground. Between her standard limp and the still-healing bruises to her torso, it was difficult. Mike casually offered his arm as added support, and she took it. Just a friend helping a friend, nothing more.

They leaned against a couple of trees, but that did little to block the freezing wind gusts.

"Looks like we're in for a lake-effect snowstorm." Annie crossed her arms, hoping to preserve her body heat.

"I hope not. The car doesn't drive well in snow. If it hits, you may need to cancel lunch with your friend so we can get home." Mike scowled as he studied the rolling dark clouds blowing in from the west.

"Is that why you don't drive it often?"

"It's part of the reason. But mostly because it draws too much attention and I like to keep a low profile."

"That's what you need," Annie said with a straight face. "Some flash to attract more business. 'Mike Edwards, PI. Let us do your digging.' Up on a billboard, with you leaning against the car, looking mysterious. Or maybe 'Let us unearth the truth.' You standing next to a tombstone holding a shovel. What do you think?"

He groaned. "Just what I don't need."

She wasn't finished teasing him. "Think about it. All the old ladies swooning over your picture and calling you to find their missing dog. Of course, that would require you to have tea at their houses so they can show you off to their friends."

"I met a guy who claimed he could do that. Find lost pets. Said there was good money in it. Do you think Jorge or Simon would be better at it?"

Annie's chuckle turned into full-blown laughter. She put one hand to her side as unused muscles complained. "Not Simon. Definitely not Simon. He's allergic to cats."

"We'll talk about it later. We have action. See the couple across the river?" Mike tipped his head in their direction.

They appeared to be older than the standard college couple, but Annie couldn't see the woman's face well enough to identify her against the old picture Kathleen's mother had provided. Mike and Annie stepped away from the cover of the trees. The couple pointed towards Annie and Mike, then headed up the incline towards the bridge.

"We passed muster." Mike muttered.

Annie hoped he was right. They seemed to be taking a long time to reappear. Had they changed their minds?

They emerged from farther down the street, approaching Mike and Annie from the rear. What were they afraid of?

"Is there anyone with you?" the man said.

"It's just the two of us, like we agreed," Annie said, slowly swiveling. "I'm assuming you are Kathleen and Aaron?"

Kathleen, a young woman with long brown hair, and Aaron, who looked slightly older than her, held a whispered conversation before Kathleen answered. "Only my mother called me Kathleen. No matter how many times I asked her to, she wouldn't call me Katy."

"Having met your mother, I'm not surprised." She held out her hand. "I'm Annie, this is Mike."

Katy grasped the offered hand and leaned in so close her breath warmed Annie's face. "Do you need rescued?" she whispered.

"What?" Annie swiveled to see Aaron walking with Mike towards the yellow Camaro.

Katy touched Annie's cheek. "These

bruises aren't fresh, but I can't imagine what they looked like when they happened."

"They were given to me by my ex. You can't see the worst of them. Mike is my boss. He saved me."

"Your ex is in jail, I hope."

Annie shook her head. "No. He's in a grave."

Katy raised her eyebrows. "Talk about drastic measures."

"It was necessary."

"I'll take your word on it." A few flakes of white whirled around them. Katy tugged her coat closed. "The snow won't hold off much longer. There's a diner down the street. Let's get coffee."

Even though it was mid-morning, the coffee shop in the outdated strip mall bustled with customers. It took a few minutes for the staff to take their order, so the four sat in silence while they waited. Katy fiddled with the jukebox, avoiding looking across the table at Annie and Mike. Annie scooted closer to Mike, trying to find a comfortable spot and avoid the ripped vinyl seat.

The bitter but welcome scent of fresh coffee arrived a second before the waitress bearing the drinks did. Annie sipped her drink before laying a manila envelope on the table.

Katy ignored it. "Tell me why my mother hired you."

Mike butted in. "She approached the agency to find you. We got a whole story about how much she misses you, and how she regretted not looking for you while your father was alive. It even included what I interpreted as fake tears. Then she didn't follow up with any of the documents we requested. Set off about a dozen red flags."

"That's what she told you. What is her real reason?"

"We don't know. Once the initial retainer was used up, we dropped the investigation," Mike explained.

"But you're here." Katy took a sip of her coffee.

"That is my doing." Annie rotated the cup in her hands, enjoying the warmth. "It bothered me how you disappeared from your parents' public life about the time you turned twelve. It was a mystery I felt compelled to solve. Mike humored my obsession and allowed me to keep digging."

Aaron wrapped his arm around Katy and tugged her closer.

Katy lowered her eyes. "It took me a year of therapy to figure it out. That's about the time I started developing, and my mother decided I'd become her competition. She shut me out emotionally, and wouldn't allow my father to go to school events or activities, either."

Annie had anticipated some form of

abuse, but not this. "That may explain this," she said, tapping the envelope.

"What is it?"

"Your father's will."

"And there it is." Katy stiffened. "You'll give me a copy for the low, low sum of how much?"

"Nada. Zero." Annie pushed it across the table. "It's yours. I got it through public records. As far as I can tell, it includes the information that you need to establish your claim. And I'm no lawyer, but I suggest you get one, based on the amounts involved."

"And you have one you'd like to suggest."

"Wrong again. The only lawyer I know in the area is the friend of my second cousin, and he deals in criminal law."

Katy reached towards the package but didn't touch it. "Why are you doing this?"

"Honestly? I believe your mother is trying to get her hands on your money. I don't want that to happen. In the little time I've dealt with her, she's done nothing to make me like her."

"In other words, you think she's a grade-A bitch." The corners of Katy's mouth wiggled.

"I'll neither confirm nor deny that."

To Annie's surprise, moisture pooled in Katy's eyes. Annie reached for a packet of tissues in her purse, but Mike was faster and handed Katy an old-fashioned white cotton handkerchief.

"Don't mind me," Katy said, dabbing at

the corner of her eyes. "You didn't tell me she's my mother and I should forgive her and let bygones be bygones. The validation is important."

She studied Annie's face. "But it makes sense you would understand."

The table fell silent while a waitress stopped by to refill their cups. When she left, Katy asked, "So, how much money are you talking about?"

Chapter Twenty-One

The snowfall hadn't ceased during the meeting in the diner and a thin coat covered Mike's car. Annie used her coat sleeve to clear the passenger-side window. "Are we going to be able to meet Joannie for lunch?" she asked. "She was looking forward to meeting you."

Mike had taken a snow brush out of his trunk and was busy clearing off the accumulated powder. "I don't think so. I'd rather get on the road. Why don't you call her and give her my apologies? There's a payphone in the diner. I'll have the car warmed up by the time you get back."

True to his word, the heater was on full blast when Annie slid into the passenger seat. The windshield wipers beat a lively tempo, keeping the snow cleared away. "That went well," she said.

"I'd put it in the win column," Mike agreed. He put the car into gear and eased out of the parking lot.

The snow was melting as fast as the flakes hit the wet pavement. Once they reached I-79, the traffic kept the travel paths cleared. Annie thought some truckers were going too fast, but trusted the drivers knew what they were doing.

Brake lights flared in front of them and Mike slowed. A State Police vehicle passed them, lights flashing and sirens blaring. Mike muttered under his breath as a little red Toyota followed too closely in their wake.

Annie put a hand on the dashboard. "They're going to cause an accident."

Mike slowed and clicked on his turn signal. "There's a Wendy's at the next exit. Let's get something to eat while the traffic settles."

She wasn't hungry, but wouldn't argue. "Sure."

More sirens screamed as they reached the turnoff. When they got to the top and turned left, Annie got a good view of the interstate, with a train of brake lights. It looked bad.

Other people had the same idea to get away from traffic, but Mike and Annie found a small table near the entrance. The perfect spot to overhear other people's conversations as they stood in line.

"That looked like a bad one."

"What were those truckers thinking?"

"It'll take forever to get it cleaned up."

Mike rose. "Wait here." He went to hold a quiet conversation with one newcomer and returned shortly.

"Change of plans. We need to find a hotel to hole up for the night. Southbound traffic won't be moving soon."

"I saw one—the brand with a red roof—

on the other side of the exit." It would be a strain on her already thin budget, but safety came first.

"And the sooner we grab rooms, the better."

His words were prophetic. In the hotel lobby, a small line waited for the front desk clerk, while the phone rang off the hook. Soon, more people joined the line.

The clerk finished his paperwork, and with weariness in his eyes, asked, "Do you have reservations?"

"No, but we're looking for two rooms. Have you got anything available?"

"We're down to one room. Single bed, but it's a queen."

"Do you have any cots?" Mike shuffled his feet.

"No. And if you want the room, you better grab it now, before someone makes a phone reservation."

"We'll make it work, Mike." Annie said, softly, "I can sleep in a chair or something. Take the room. It's better than sitting in traffic."

"If you don't want it, one of the folks behind you will," the clerk pointed out.

Mike nodded. "We'll take it."

He filled out the standard forms, and the clerk handed him two room keys and a photocopied map.

"There's a drugstore down the street if you want to pick up some essentials, and a couple of fast-food places. That and the typical waffle restaurant. Or you could get into Meadville by back streets and get a better selection of food. Local forecasts predict this storm band will get worse before it gets better, so I'd suggest sticking close by."

"I appreciate the tip." Mike jerked his head towards the line behind them. "Good luck."

The clerk raised an eyebrow. "Thanks."

Room 205 was near the elevator and the ice machine. Not the most appealing location, but it was warm and clean. Still, the vague odor of cigarette smoke met her nose when Mike opened the door. She crossed the room and tried to open the window, but was sealed closed. It faced the interstate and Annie stood there, watching the traffic not move. She avoided looking at the bed and its floral cover.

Mike patted the padded chair in the corner. "I've slept on worse," he said.

"Don't be silly. We're adults. The bed is big enough for us to each take a side." Annie turned and studied the furniture. "We can do it the old-fashioned way and put the spare blanket between us if you're afraid I'm going to attack you."

She looked up to see him grinning. "What?"

"I'm enjoying your newfound sense of humor, that's all." Mike didn't stop smiling.

"Ian hated it. Said it made me look stupid."

Annie smiled back. "I have to be careful that I don't allow it to get me in trouble."

At the drugstore, they stocked up on what they thought they'd need — toothbrushes, toothpaste, snacks, and what sleepwear they found. Annie added in a paperback Western as a distraction. Ian had tossed her collection one night when he was upset with her.

The afternoon was spent with Mike on the phone with Betty, the weather channel on the TV, and Annie wrapped up in the story of cowboys, mountains and deserts. With the toss of a coin, they ended up at the pancake house for supper.

The place was half-full. They took a table near the back, gave their orders to the young waitress, then sat and waited for their food.

"College student, you think?" Annie asked. It was an occupational hazard she'd slipped into — trying to figure out the life stories of random people.

"Yep." Mike had his back to the front of the place, but had taken a good look at the girl when she had brought their coffee.

"What subject? Teaching?"

"No, art student. I saw some paint on one arm and glitter in her hair."

"I missed that," Annie grimaced.

"You were on the wrong side," he grinned. "Definitely not a musician. I didn't see any callouses on her fingers."

"And not married. She probably works here to help pay tuition."

"Agreed. Anything else?"

"She has a boyfriend."

"And what evidence do you have?" Mike asked, leaning back.

"The faint remains of a hickey on her neck. Her collar covered most of it, but it was there."

"Good catch."

Annie added creamer to her cup of hot chocolate. "Her necklace was a gift. I can't imagine wearing jewelry like that to work in a place like this unless someone special gave it to me." She stiffened. "Trouble up front."

"What's going on?" Mike asked, tense and alert.

"A low-life just walked in the door and is giving the waitress a bad time."

"Ex-boyfriend?"

"Don't think so. Maybe a druggie running on empty. She's headed towards the cash register and looks nervous. But so does he."

Mike shifted and leaned forward so his gun was no longer pushed against the back of the booth. He edged towards the end of the bench seat. "Feel like finding out what's going on?"

"Yes. Especially since he just grabbed the necklace and jerked it off her neck. But I don't have a weapon. Mine are locked up in your office."

"I can fix that." He knocked his fork off the table and reached down with a napkin to pick it up. When he sat back up, Annie caught the glint of metal under the napkin. Not the fork. It was the small Beretta she'd seen him use in target practice. It soon nestled in her hand.

Together, they rose and, with Mike in the lead, strolled the short distance towards the front of the restaurant. They didn't want to alarm the other customers. "Something I can help you with?" he asked the tearful waitress. Annie edged around him to get behind the intruder.

"Just go back to your table and you won't get hurt," snarled the scrawny man. "But leave your wallet here."

"You've been watching too many bad movies," Mike said quietly. Annie spotted the outline of a round cylinder in the thief's coat pocket. Then Mike's gun was in his hand so quickly Annie almost missed the move that put it there. "I suggest you give the lady her necklace back."

The thug stiffened, and he took a step backward. Annie pressed the Beretta into his back. "Take your hand out of your pocket slowly," she ordered. "And put both of them on the counter."

He didn't obey. He swiveled and dashed for the door. Mike was on top of him in a heartbeat and took him to the floor. Annie turned into crowd control when other customers stood and rushed to the front. The fight was short-lived because an off-duty cop also eating supper flashed his badge to Annie, joined in the fracas, and secured the suspect with his handcuffs.

"Not your night," the officer, a middle-aged man, commented as he began his pat down of the detainee.

"He's hiding what may be a weapon in his right-hand coat pocket," Mike said. "He's got the waitress's necklace on him. And knowing his type, there's a needle stashed somewhere."

"You a cop?"

"Ex. Out of Pittsburgh. Currently, the owner of The Edwards PI Agency." Mike held out his hand. "Mike Edwards. This is one of my agents, C.T. McGregor."

The cop nodded to Annie as he shook Mike's hand. "Thanks for your assistance." He resumed his search and pulled an iron pipe out of the subject's coat.

He held up a necklace next. "This yours, Miss?" he asked.

"Yes, that's mine." The waitress put her hand to her neck.

Mike took the necklace from the officer, looked it over, and passed it to the waitress. "Here you go," he said. "A good jeweler should be able to fix the chain."

Sirens wailed in the distance.

"Why don't you two return to your seats?" the officer suggested. "We'll need to get your info for the report. I've got this covered."

Stepping carefully through the snow-covering the sidewalk, Annie and Mike returned to the hotel around 10 o'clock. Once in the room, Mike sat in the one chair while Annie perched on the bed.

"You want the bathroom?" she asked.

"Ladies first." Mike took off his shoes. "I can wait."

He'd placed the spare blanket and pillow in the easy chair when Annie came out. She opened her mouth to protest.

"The bed is yours," he said. "Don't argue with me."

She turned on the TV and rearranged the pillows on the bed when he disappeared into the bathroom. Annie considered moving the bedding back to the bed, but then she and Mike would fight about it. And she would lose. She didn't need all the pillows, so she added another one to his stack.

Once Annie changed into the oversize t-shirt she planned to sleep in, she crawled under the covers. The gravity of the situation struck her. If she was one of the guys, there'd be no insinuation about anything unethical going on. It was her responsibility to protect Mike's integrity.

She was half-asleep when Mike emerged

from the bathroom wearing a pair of loose sleep pants and a t-shirt. "Thanks for showing me a good time tonight," she said, pulling the blanket around her shoulders. "You're a pleasure to work with."

He chuckled. "I do what I can. Now, go to sleep, Ms. McGregor. I've got the alarm set for six. I want to get on the road early."

"Good night, Mr. Edwards." Annie hoped she'd get some sleep. She didn't have her nighttime meds with her.

The nightmares were standard, and this one was a repeat. Ian yelling at her about some trivial mistake—the mashed potatoes didn't have enough butter in them—that escalated to blows. A casual slap, pulling her hair, nothing that would leave permanent marks. She knew she was whimpering, but wasn't awake enough to stop.

She stiffened as two powerful arms wrapped around her, holding her tightly. She tried to push them away, but they didn't budge.

"It's okay, Annie," Mike said in a deep voice. "I've got you. You're safe."

Was this a new ending to the nightmare? Her brain training her to realize Ian was truly gone? She didn't fight the feeling of being safe and snuggled deeper into the warm chest. A delightful dream.

Chapter Twenty-Two

Neither Annie nor Mike spoke during the long trip back to Pittsburgh. Mike had the excuse that he needed to concentrate on the slushy roads and heavy traffic. Annie didn't have an excuse.

She'd blown it. Oh, Mike wouldn't fire her, but their working relationship would never be the same. The aftermath of the nightmare would hang over their heads, like a storm cloud ready to burst open and wreak destruction.

Mike pulled up in front of her apartment building. Some days, the brick building seemed to welcome her, but today it looked old and worn. The thin layer of snow on the empty flowerpots was already coated with coal soot.

"You can get an early start to the weekend," he said. "I don't have anything urgent for you today."

"We're going to have to talk about it sometime," Annie said.

He blinked. His chest rose and fell as he contemplated the windshield. "We are. But not now. We're both tired and may say things we'll regret later."

Annie opened the car door. "I'll see you on Monday."

"Monday," he nodded. "See you then."

Halfway up the stairs, Annie realized he'd

left. Hadn't followed her inside, checked her apartment, or imposed any of the other safety protocols. Not that they were needed anymore; Ian was dead. The only claim he had on her was her memories.

Time to create new ones.

The neighborhood bar was busy, but the old vets made room for her at their table. She nursed her one beer, knowing it had to last since her medical issues had required abstinence. But the guys kept her entertained with stories of other bar patrons so she didn't miss the alcohol buzz.

Halfway through the evening, Ace and Sam waved towards the front door. Annie was engrossed in one of Cap'n's tales. She didn't expect that another chair would be added to the table next to hers, and that Coulson would fill that spot. He casually draped his arm over her shoulders.

"Celebrating, Annie?" he asked as he set his whiskey glass on the table. "Shouldn't Mike be here?"

"You talked to Owen?" Annie avoided the question. She'd called Owen earlier to thank him for helping her.

"He checks in daily."

"And you assumed I'd be here?"

Coulson grinned. "I checked your apartment's parking lot first. And your car was there, so I made a wild guess and here I am. Simple PI work."

"I've become predictable. That's not good." She'd lived the last few years not settling down, to make it harder for Ian to track her. She didn't need to do that anymore.

"The job will change that. If Mike isn't giving you enough to do, hit me up."

She tapped his arm, still resting across her shoulders. "If I worked for you, you couldn't do this."

"True." Coulson didn't change positions. "But it's fun to make Mike believe I'm trying to poach you."

"Why do you enjoy antagonizing him so much?"

He ruffled her hair. "You picked up on that, eh? Here's the scoop. I may have the bigger and more successful company, but Mike is a better investigator. I've learned a lot from him. You stick with him, and you'll be better than me. I enjoy taking him down a peg or two, so he doesn't get a swelled head. But don't worry, I'm not using you to get to him. I like you, Annie McGregor."

"Don't push your luck." He'd been playing by her rules, but she still wasn't sure about where she wanted the relationship to go. She might be almost healed physically from her trauma, but her emotions had a long way to go.

He drained his glass, then picked up Annie's mug. "We're both due for a refill."

Annie let him.

Later, he walked her to her door to make sure she got there safely. She considered inviting him in.

"May I see you in my office?" Mike stood in front of her desk. She hadn't heard him coming because she'd been typing up the collection letters, before printing them for Betty to mail out. It was a convoluted process, but made Betty feel like she was still useful for doing more than answering the phone.

Annie didn't want to put off the confrontation. "I'll be there as soon as I finish."

"Sooner would be better. I have a meeting in fifteen minutes." He turned on one foot and marched back to his office.

Did he believe fifteen minutes would be enough? Had he convinced himself that what had happened wasn't important? Or was he going to avoid discussing the incident and talk about something else?

She finished the letter and printed it, adding it to the stack she'd already completed. Then copied it to the floppy disk so Mike could access a copy if he needed. She still hadn't quite gotten Mike to understand the process, but he'd get there eventually.

With the disk in her hand, Annie headed to Mike's office, rehashing planned responses. Did she apologize? Pretend she didn't remember? Throw herself in Mike's arms and hope he'd kiss her?

What deep, dark corner of her brain had come up with that? Whatever, it needed to crawl back to its hole and stay there.

She knocked on his door frame.

"Come in and shut the door behind you," Mike said, without looking up from the paperwork he held. "Have a seat."

She laid the disk on his desk. "What's up?"

He still didn't look at her. "How long have you been having nightmares?"

"Ian laughed when I had them. After my accident, they eased up, probably because of the meds I was taking. They came back after my encounter with Ian when he was released from jail."

"Are you talking to a shrink?"

"I can't afford one. I've been trying to save up my money to pay the hospital bills." Annie rubbed her palms on her knees.

"Didn't anyone tell you? The bill has been taken care of." Mike finally raised his head to meet her eyes. "I expected the hospital to inform you."

"You don't have that kind of money. Who paid?"

Mike shrugged. "I had nothing to do with it."

"Who paid, Mike?"

"Dan Russell."

"What?"

"I had the same reaction." One side of Mike's mouth rose. "I'm not sure who reached out to him. Mother Hilary claims it wasn't her."

"Eliminating possible suspects?" Annie grinned.

"I had to call in a favor to even find out who made the payment. Then I hit a dead end. But that should give you some wiggle room in your budget, and one less thing to worry about."

"And you paid me even when I wasn't working."

"I'd do it for any of the guys. It's my policy. This job has enough hazards that I don't want anyone worrying about getting hurt while on duty." Mike pushed his chair away from his desk. "But that brings up another concern."

"Which is?"

Mike unlocked his file cabinet. "I planned to give your guns back. Now, I'm not sure."

"You believe I might use them during a nightmare?" Was he right? If she grabbed one of her guns while fighting off Ian's ghost, would she fire it at some innocent person?

"It crossed my mind. But if I'm going to

return you to full duty, you need to have them available."

Excitement surged in Annie's chest. "You have a case for me?"

"Nothing major." Mike picked up a file and shoved it over the desk. "Another potential cheating husband. A few late nights should wrap it up."

Annie flipped through the file. "It looks pretty easy. A story as old as they come. A husband hiring a hot young secretary and sleeping with her."

"While his devoted wife of fifteen years stays home with their two children, one boy and one girl." Mike shook his head. "No shady bars for this case. Normal business attire will suffice for the lunchtime meetings."

"Was the wife able to give you a list of restaurants her husband goes to?"

"You can ask her yourself." Mike glanced at his watch. "She should be here in five minutes."

Annie had always wanted to go to Froggy's. The dark interior and high wooden booths made it a perfect spot for a clandestine meeting. Or any business meeting, based on the number of suits that filled the surrounding seats.

She'd followed Mr. Garrett, a tall, dark

and handsome middle-aged man, and his secretary into the restaurant, but had been seated several tables away. That made it impossible to keep an eye on their interactions. She'd have to make a trip to the restroom to get an incriminating photo or two, and prove the couple was doing more than eating together.

To spare the client's slim budget, she settled on soup and salad for lunch. No alcohol for her. She couldn't see if the couple was enjoying a glass of wine with their lunch or not. She wouldn't be able to resolve the case in her first attempt but she was back in the game.

The next day, Wednesday, they ended up at Gandy's Dancer. The setup of the tables made it easier for Annie to track their behavior. All the body language was there—holding hands, leaning into one another—but nothing crossed the line. There were no kisses, and they sat on opposite sides of the table. The case wasn't turning out to be the slam dunk Annie had expected.

She'd gained one important piece of information—the secretary's name. She'd called the main office and asked for an appointment to meet with Mr. Garrett. Her son, Donny, was working on a school project and wanted to interview the manager of the procurement department. The call was shuttled through to Mr. Garrett's office, and she and Erica Densmore had a wonderful conversation about the non-existent

Donny. Who never showed up for the interview, of course.

Thursday, the couple didn't leave for lunch. And left for home at separate times. Had they been tipped off that they were being followed?

"I'm worried, Mike," she told him via walkie-talkie. "He's been going straight home and not leaving."

"Do you want to borrow my car tomorrow?" he suggested.

"Yes. Although, according to Mrs. Garrett, he comes home early on Fridays."

The walkie-talkie crackled. "Fridays are a traditional day to take a long lunch."

Annie had never worked a job that allowed that practice. "I'll take your word for it."

"Try switching your outfit, too. Wear a dress instead of pants." Mike said. "Do you have a flowery one?"

She didn't, but it was easy enough to make a quick trip to a secondhand store. Although it might be hard to find a dress suitable for the season, a matching sweater would complete the outfit. Add a pair of cute shoes, and she'd pass for a lower-level executive secretary.

Friday morning, when she showed up at the office, Betty checked her out approvingly. "Looking good. But why? I thought this was just a standard assignment."

"It is. This was Mike's suggestion."

"Too bad he's not here to see it." Betty held up Mike's keys. "As usual, I'm not sure where he is, but he left these."

Annie nodded. "We're switching vehicles. But when did he leave?"

Betty shrugged. "He was gone when I got here. Standard operating procedure for him."

Annie almost missed Garrett when he left the building with a group of other employees, including Erica, the secretary. She and Garrett made a good-looking couple, both about the same height, with dark hair, hers was waist-length.\. Even though they walked side-by-side, they didn't touch, leaving Annie doubting the case. Or were they just good at hiding from their coworkers?

They left in different cars. Annie hung back, making sure that all the vehicles headed the same direction. Which they did. They ended up at an Eat'n Park.

"All dressed up and nowhere to go," Annie muttered. Between the normal lunch crowd and the new group, her chances of getting a table were slim to none. And it would be suspicious if she sat in the restaurant's parking lot the entire time.

But there were several businesses across

the road where she could park and use binoculars to maintain contact with her subjects. What sparked her interest is that there were several motels a block away. The perfect opportunity for Garrett and Erica.

Annie's stomach growled, and she dug into the bag of snacks she'd brought along. The peanut butter crackers would hold her over until she got a more substantial meal. Which might be as late as supper, depending on what happened in the next hour.

It was fifty minutes later when the group began filtering out. Annie assumed they'd had the buffet. But neither Garrett nor Erica was among the first ones leaving. Annie munched on another cracker and waited.

The couple were among the last to leave. Annie had the engine running and was set to follow them when they showed up in the doorway. They'd have to go away from the hotels on the one way, and pull a u-turn at the light. She'd pulled a penny from the cupholder and flipped it. Heads. The hotels won.

Luck was with her. Garrett made the needed turn, and Annie confirmed Erica was with him. And no one else. They made the needed turn and ended up in the parking lot of the better hotel. Annie used the side street to get there without dealing with the traffic that clogged the main street.

They didn't hold hands as they walked

into the hotel lobby. Annie snapped a few pictures, then parked. She entered, and stopped by the rack of fliers for local attractions. As the couple checked in, she took a few more pictures with the camera Coulson had given her.

It was all the case file needed. She couldn't enter the couple's room and catch them in the act.

"What I did," she reported to Mike later, "Was stop at the front desk and ask questions about rates when my mother visits in a few weeks. Smiled my prettiest and flirted. God, I am out of practice. Anyway, when he went to the back to grab towels for another guest, I set my purse on the desk. With luck, I snapped a picture of Garrett's registration card, which wasn't put away. Of course, I stuck around the hotel until they left."

"Hand over your film. I'll get the pictures processed tonight. I'll know by tomorrow if you've got enough to satisfy the client. Good job, Annie." Mike's smile spread from ear to ear as he held out his hand.

She'd finally done something right. The other guys might complain about cheating cases, but she felt as if she'd finally proven herself.

"By the way, I like the outfit." Mike laid the film canisters on his desk. "I can see it being useful in other investigations."

It was irrational, but for a moment, Annie had hoped that Mike had seen her as something beyond one of his workers. "Let me know if they turn out," she said, biting back her disappointment.

"If not, we have a baseline for further surveillance. Like I said, good job. There'll be a bonus in your paycheck if Mrs. Garrett is satisfied."

Annie didn't want to be alone. "Care to join me in a celebration?" she asked.

"I would," he said. "But I promised Simon I'd back him up tonight. Twice now, the man he's following has slipped away."

Was that a look of regret on his face? Or was Annie imagining things?

"Good luck," she said.

He put her keys on the top of his desk. "Another time, Annie."

Annie didn't want to be alone. Although she hadn't finished reading it, the book she'd bought the night of the snowstorm didn't call out to her. She didn't want to go to the local bar, either. She wanted to swap stories with other PIs and pretend her life was normal. Average.

The light flashed on her answering machine. Annie was tempted to ignore it, assuming it was her mother. Who else would call her?

But duty called, and she pushed the button to listen to the message. "Hey, girl," Coulson's voice said. "We're going out to celebrate closing a case tonight. Wanna come along? Give me a buzz."

A little Coulson in her life sounded like what she needed.

Chapter Twenty-Three

Mike laid a thick folder on her desk. "Are you ready to try this again?"

Annie lifted an eyebrow. "Try what?"

"The Hansens. Leona has come up with another retainer. She has no new information, but she's sure he's up to something." He patted the folder. "What have we overlooked?."

"I think she's right, but I'm worried he's seen me a few too many times. I need to come up with a disguise." Annie ran a lock of her straight hair through her fingers. "Curls?"

He gently tilted her face up and studied it. "It might work. Or dying it red. A wig might be a better choice, although none of the ones you already own. Right now, your hair is perfect for being anonymous and you shouldn't change it."

Annie had thought they were having a non-work connection. Wrong again. "Time to go shopping."

"You can expense the wig." Mike ran his hand over his head. "This is new to me. All the guys need to do is switch baseball caps."

"Wait until I hit you up for makeup," Annie grinned.

"Are you taking Owen along on your surveillance? Or should I be your backup?"

Annie hesitated. Was he being supportive,

or did he still not trust her? "I'd love to work with you, Mike, but this will require Owen's talents. Or are you a pickpocket on top of all your other skills?"

Mike held up one hand and spread out his fingers. "These paws are way too big for the fine work he does."

Annie had a flash of the things he could do with those powerful hands. She ducked her head so he wouldn't see the red rising in her cheeks. "Right. And that's why I have to do this with Owen."

"I'll give Coulson a call and set it up."

The Outlaw was busy, but not crowded. Owen fit in well, in his old jeans and a George Strait t-shirt. The red, curly wig Annie wore drew a few too many eyes for her to feel anonymous, and that wasn't good.

With Willie Nelson playing in the background, Owen posed as the perfect boyfriend, keeping his arm wrapped around her waist, except when he was getting her a drink refill. As they'd planned, he backed her up against a wall so she could monitor Hansen without being obvious. Hansen didn't have his normal companions with him, and Annie worried that the night would be a washout.

Owen leaned in and whispered in her ear. "Where is he?"

Her hips swaying as if they were dancing, Annie swiveled him around so he could see the room near the back door. "There."

"Do you want me to make a stab at it?"

"I'll let you make the call."

He winked. "Hold my drink, darlin'. I'll be right back."

Annie tracked his path towards the restrooms. He wove through the bar, a grinning fool who'd had too much to drink. He bumped into Hansen on his way, but his hands stayed in sight.

"Does your friend have a brother?" asked a woman hanging out nearby.

Annie had to drag her eyes away from Owen. "Sorry, he's one of a kind. He's got several sisters, though, if you swing that way."

The woman, a mousy blonde, giggled. "No, but thanks. I'd go to the Exile for that scene."

Annie might need the information for another case another time, so she kept the conversation going. She'd lost track of Owen, but wasn't worried about her safety. "I've never heard of that one."

"Little bar. Out towards the airport. Great place to go for a girls' night out."

Then Owen slipped his arm around her waist. "Miss me?" He planted a loud kiss on her cheek.

She handed him his beer. "Did everything come out okay?"

"You can find out later." He winked at the blonde. "Thanks for keeping her company, but we have to go now."

He drained his beer and reached for her still half-full mug.

"So soon?" Annie protested.

"I have to work tomorrow, remember?"

She gave the blonde a little wave. "Nice talking to you."

Outside, they continued their charade, holding hands, in case anyone was watching. Annie seethed with excitement, but Owen remained calm during the walk. He'd tell her what he'd found when the time was right.

"Well?" she asked as they got in the car and fastened their seatbelts.

"Wait," Owen said. "I want to make sure we aren't followed."

It must be good. Annie peered into the sideview mirror, but there were too many cars and too many headlights for her to track any one vehicle. He pulled into the parking lot of a furniture store about a mile away and unfastened his seatbelt. Then he undid the snap on his jeans.

"Want to see what I've got in here?" he asked in a deep voice.

Annie swatted him on the shoulder. "Don't play Coulson. It doesn't suit you."

"So, the rumors are true. He's met his match and hasn't seduced you." Owen chuckled as he pulled a small plastic square from his pants.

"Where did Hansen have it?" she asked, reaching for it.

Owen handed it over. "It wasn't on him. I found it in the restroom, wrapped in plastic and taped to the inside of the toilet's water tank."

"Well, that sucks. We have no proof that Hansen had anything to do with it." Annie tapped the disk with her forefinger.

"We'll have to try again another night," Owen said.

Annie laid the disk on the dashboard. "I'll check it later for clues, but I don't expect to find anything. My computer might not be able to read it, anyway."

"Got it. You're the expert. I'll take you home."

Annie's keyboard echoed in the empty office as she finished the last report. The disk sat on her desk, haunting her. As busy as the phone had been, Annie hadn't had time to deal with it. She wanted to give it her uninterrupted attention.

At five, Annie turned on the answering machine and considered going home. But the disk taunted her. She might get lucky, and the computer would open it up to a simple letter.

She stuck it in the proper slot and waited while the computer churned and tried to decipher the information. Nothing happened.

But Annie wasn't done. She could find out what files were on the disk with a simple command. DIR. The resulting list confused her. It was short, only 8 files. It shouldn't take long to find out if her computer would read them.

She opened the first one, but didn't understand what she was seeing. It looked like a grainy photo, but she didn't know what it was a picture of. Lots of shadows and dark spots. She closed it and tried the next file.

It was clearer. What appeared to be a child, maybe seven or eight, sitting on a bed. With their back to the camera and no shirt on. Annie couldn't tell if the child was wearing shorts or not.

Weird. She opened the third file. And the fourth. Like one of those old flip books, the pictures changed only a little. At the sixth file, an adult entered the scene. The seventh picture revealed the man naked and aroused. The eighth picture had Annie running for the restroom. She made it in time to throw up in the sink. Several times. Until her stomach was empty and she was left with dry heaves.

"Annie." Then Mike was holding her, pulling her hair away from her face. "Annie, what's wrong? Do I need to take you to the ER?"

She ran the water to flush the remains of her distress down the drain. "No ER," she said as she splashed water on her face.

"What's going on?" he asked, smoothing her hair.

"It's worse than bad." She spat into the sink, trying to clear the remnants of vomit from her mouth. "It's on my computer."

As she leaned against the sink, she wished he hadn't left. It took forever before he came back.

"Where did that trash come from?" he asked, his voice rough.

"The other night. When Owen and I followed Hansen. It wasn't on him. Owen found it taped to the toilet in the men's room." Annie swallowed hard, fighting back another dry heave.

"That means the police can't do anything with it."

"What the hell is it, Mike?"

"We need to have a long conversation." Mike's cheeks reddened. "But not here. Go home. I'll bring supper and meet you there."

Annie stared out the window of her apartment but found no comfort there. Nothing but blackness. She'd already made one trip to the bathroom for a moment of dry heaves while waiting for Mike. A knock on the door broke her out of her dark contemplation.

She left the security chain on and peeked through the gap. Mike stood there, carrying several bags. She closed the door and wondered if she was ready for this. If she'd ever be ready. She slid the bolt and let him in.

He nodded, but neither spoke. He carried the bags to her kitchen and upoacked them. More boxes of Chinese food than the two of them could eat in one sitting, and a fifth of Jack. He took two mismatched coffee cups out of the cupboard, set them on the table, and poured an equal amount of whiskey into each.

Mike picked up both cups and handed one to Annie. "This isn't a sipping situation. Bottoms up."

She didn't protest and upended the cup. The harsh liquid burned all the way down. "You trying to get me drunk, Mike?" She coughed as the whiskey settled in her stomach.

"Absolutely." He set plates and silverware on the table. "First, we need to get some food in your stomach. And don't give me any grief about not wanting to eat. We both need this."

Hadn't Mike seen everything?

As if they were on a date in an upscale restaurant, Mike pulled out one of her beat-up kitchen chairs and held it out for her. She took her seat and waited for his next move.

He poured them each another shot and

sat across from her. "Dig in," he said.

Annie took small servings from several of the boxes, paying no attention to what they were and, ignoring the chopsticks, picked at the fried rice with her fork.

"Eat, Annie," Mike growled.

She still didn't feel like eating. But she didn't want to disappoint Mike. Swallowing the first few bites was hard, but with the aid of the whiskey, each bite got easier. She was on her second plate and fourth shot—it still burned in her throat when she gathered the courage to ask, "What are we dealing with, Mike?"

He stared at the ceiling. "Kiddie porn. Fuckin' kiddie porn."

Chapter Twenty-Four

The light bulb over the kitchen table flickered. Annie downed the Jack left in her cup and pushed her plate away. She'd had enough. Mike splashed more whiskey into each of their cups.

"When I was on the force, we'd hear stories, but none of us actually handled a case. I can't tell you about the surrounding areas. There were always rumors, but that's all they were. Rumors." Mike dropped his fork, and it clattered against the cheap ceramic plate. "Fucking child pornography. I never thought I'd deal with it."

"But why? Why would anyone want to see…" Annie didn't say the words.

"It's a sad reality. Granted, the perpetrators are mostly men. But the underground films…you don't want to know what happens in those films." Mike lifted his cup to his mouth. "Who ever thought of using a computer?"

He'd need a taxi to go home. Or spend the night. "Do we go to the police in the morning?" Annie asked.

"How bad do you want to nail Hansen if he's involved in this?"

She didn't have much to give up. "I'd pass on every penny of Mrs. Hansen's retainer to figure out who's responsible for that atrocity."

Mike nodded. "It may come down to that. From this moment on, we don't share information with anyone else. Not Betty, not any of the guys, not Owen or Coulson. We don't discuss the case in the office. It's just me and you. We can't risk word getting out and getting to the people responsible."

"If you say so."

"We need a code word." Mike poured himself another shot. "A signal we can use in case we need to get someplace private to talk."

Annie tapped her middle finger on the table. "Soot. It's as black and smelly as this case."

"That's a good one." Mike held his cup in the air. "Let's drink to that."

Definitely feeling the alcohol, she clunked her cup against his and giggled. "So, what's our next step?"

"The suspects will be riled up when they realize the disk is missing. I expect they'll move the base of their activities. Where do you think they'll go?"

"Eliminate The Outlaw. Not the disco club. That was a one-time thing. And not the Chinese restaurant, because the layout is too open. I'd consider the little movie shop. They may use it to exchange VHS tapes." She ticked off each location on her fingers. "I assume they put this shit on VCR?"

Mike nodded. "I'd like to get pictures of their customers. If this case develops into something, it'll give the cops a list of potential co-conspirators."

"That'll take a lot of man-hours, but I'm not working any other cases, so that job falls to me. You have to keep the agency running." Annie took another sip of the Jack. She'd grown accustomed to the harshness. "I want to see if they have 'special' customers that come before or after regular business hours."

"You'll need to check in at the office to make everything appear normal, and we'll need to switch cars." Mike poured himself another shot or more of the Jack.

"If any of the houses across the street are empty, we could use one as a lookout."

"Check it out. You might get lucky."

Annie realized the phrase had another connotation, but she was too engrossed in the details of the current endeavor to pursue it. "Can I get into the back room? I bet that's where the action is."

He shook his head. "Too risky. I don't want any possibility of contact."

"I'm tempted to drive to the store right now and see what I can see." Annie upended her cup and set it back on the table with a thunk.

"Where are your car keys?" Mike asked.

Annie blinked. "In my purse. Why?"

He held out his hand. "You aren't going anywhere tonight. Hand them over."

What was good for the goose was good

for the gander. "I can say the same for you."

They stared at each other until Annie stood, went to her bedroom, grabbed a large metal box, and brought it to the table. She shoved aside food containers to make room for it. "Keys. Yours and mine. In there. Guns, too. The key will be in the cupboard."

A slow smile spread across Mike's face. "Are you holding me hostage?"

"The local cops have a reputation for stopping folks for the slightest suspicion of drunk driving. You, my friend, fit that category." She tapped the box. "So, keys in here. Guns, too."

He dropped the keys in the box, not denying the accusation. "Why the guns?"

"I woke up from a nightmare with a gun in my hand one too many times." Annie crunched her mouth. "It seemed like a good precaution."

"Smart move." He stood. In slow motion, he took his gun out of his shoulder harness and put it in the box. He planted his right foot on his chair, then raised his pants leg and unbuckled his Beretta. "I wouldn't want you to shoot me in my sleep. With my own revolver."

Was it her imagination, or did he lift his pants leg higher than normal and take longer than usual to remove the gun? She didn't think he was *that* drunk. "Ha. I get the feeling no one can sneak up on you." Annie had removed her shoulder harness before eating and it was hanging on the back of her chair. She took out her weapon and added it to the box.

Mike raised his eyebrows. "Where are the rest?"

"In my purse."

"Well?"

"Hold on," Annie grumbled. She grabbed her purse off the easy chair in the front room, dug out her keys and derringer, and dropped them in the box. "Better?"

"Now we're even. Lock it up. Where do you keep it?"

As she turned the key, she realized there weren't many places in the little apartment to stash anything valuable. "Top shelf of the cupboard on the right."

Mike put it in the designated spot. "Mother Hubbard's cupboard. I haven't seen one this bare since the last time I looked in mine."

"I live as if Ian could reappear and take everything away."

The cupboard door banged as he slammed it shut. "He's never coming back. I made sure of that."

And there it was. She'd suspected that Mike was responsible for the shot that killed Ian, and the cops had covered for him. Annie tapped her forehead. "I know that up here, but it'll take a long time to sink in."

"Now I know what to get you for Christmas." He looked around the room.

Annie followed his gaze and realized how stark it appeared. Nothing marked the space as her haven. No artwork, no flowers, no pillows on the couch. "Decorating hasn't been my priority."

"I'm not criticizing you, Annie. Some days I wonder why I maintain an apartment at all. I'm never there."

"You need a spot to store your cars." Annie chuckled. She'd definitely had too much to drink. Still, she finished what was left in her cup.

Mike's lips wiggled. "Ouch. The truth hurts." He added more Jack to both cups.

Annie shook her head. "I'm done."

"Will you be able to sleep tonight?"

She yawned. "I don't think I have a choice."

"Then go to bed. Just point me to your spare blankets. The couch looks comfortable enough." Mike covered his mouth as he yawned, too.

Did she have a spare blanket? Or pillow? Annie panicked. She could give him the one off her bed and use the afghan that served as a bedspread. "I'll get them for you."

"Don't go to any trouble. I've slept worse places."

She knew about the cot he kept in a closet at work. Everyone did. And everybody pretended they didn't. "My bed is a single, but I'm open to sharing."

Had those words really left her mouth? They hung in the air, and Annie's checks burned.

"You've had too much to drink, and that's my fault." Mike reached out and tilted her head. "I appreciate the invite, Annie, but I'm still your boss, and I won't take advantage of you."

She pulled away. "Let me get you that blanket and pillow."

In the bedroom, Annie leaned her forehead against the wall, taking a moment to recover her equilibrium. She'd made a fool of herself. At least she could blame it on the whiskey.

With her blanket slung over her arm, and carrying her pillow, she returned to the front room. "Here you go," she said, shoving them at Mike.

"Don't be mad at me. Your offer is tempting, but I can't take you up on it. When you aren't drunk, you'll see that." Mike took the bedding without touching her.

She wasn't upset with him; she was mad at herself. "You want to use the bathroom first?"

"No, you go."

She'd been dismissed.

Annie snuggled into her afghan as she came to full wakefulness, the weight of it comforting. The sun shone through her closed curtains, and she couldn't figure out the time, and why her alarm hadn't gone off.

Memories flooded back, along with a roaring headache.. She wasn't sure which was worse—the pounding in her skull, the discovery of the porn, or Mike's rejection. The decision was easy.

Hansen had to go down.

After a week of the stakeout, Annie had avoided Mike each time she dropped off an additional roll of film at the office. Even the exchange of cars was done through Betty. Annie had identified over two hundred customers, logged in a notebook by date, time, and description. Hardly enough to keep the business going. There were repeats, and she confirmed five men were previously associated with Hansen .

But Hansen hadn't shown up during her vigil. She wished she could have maintained a watch over his home as well, to figure out what he was doing. But the stakeout served a larger purpose, she reminded herself as she took pictures of an elderly couple going into the video store. They didn't seem like potential suspects, but she dutifully added them to the log.

Even with her coat buttoned, and wrapped in a blanket, she found in the back seat of Mike's car, she shivered. It had been a long day, and the temperature was dropping. Snow fell in spurts, coating the windshield. Annie couldn't run her wipers without giving herself away. She wondered if the weather would bring a rush of customers looking for a distraction to fill the evening or send everyone home.

A small truck pulled into the lot beside her. Her truck. The one Mike was driving. She stared out the window, waiting for Mike to make his move.

He opened the passenger door, set her camera and purse on the floor, and slid in. "Any luck?" he asked.

"Nothing new."

Annie tugged the blanket around her as they sat in silence.

"We need to talk," Mike finally said.

"Do you want an update on the case? I've been leaving you messages." Annie didn't look in his direction.

"And I've been reading them. But that's not what I mean."

She bit the bullet. "I put you in an uncomfortable situation and I'm sorry."

"No. It's the other way around. What were you supposed to believe when I practically did a striptease taking off my weapons?"

"Wait. You tried to seduce me and then backed down?" That's why it had been easy to avoid him. He'd been avoiding her, too.

He shook his head. "No. It wasn't like that.

I was treating you like I'd treat any of the guys. But you aren't one of the guys, and I'm clueless when it comes to you."

"None of the guys has ever propositioned you?" she asked, half-serious.

"I didn't say that." Mike chuckled. "He no longer works for me. I didn't fire him, but he decided being a PI wasn't his cup of tea."

"It's not for everyone," she agreed.

"Is it for you, Annie?"

Honesty was the best policy. "I don't know yet. I feel like I'm not good enough. If we nail Hansen, I might change my mind."

"That's fair. You've had a rough start in the business." He wiped the fog from the side window.

"The cops made their once-a-night trip through the neighborhood," Annie said to fill the silence that followed. "The store should shut down soon. Not that we'll be able to see it."

He nodded. "Time to head home. Do you want to trade cars?"

That made sense. "If anyone is watching us, we've already been made." She shrugged off the blanket and folded it before returning it to the back seat.

"Don't come back tomorrow if this weather holds up. You won't be able to conceal yourself." As he opened the door, a blast of cold wind rattled the car. "Stay home if the roads get bad."

Chapter Twenty-Five

Computers were good for more than writing letters. Annie entered the list of video shop customers into a database and sorted the information, trying to find a pattern. Only one man stuck out. He was in the store every day. Annie couldn't invent a reason for him to be there, and staying for hours.

She wondered if Owen could get his hands on the store records, so she would have a list of names to try to match with faces. But this operation was strictly between her and Mike. He'd warned her about not tampering with files that police investigators might need.

Which meant she hadn't touched the disk, either. She'd locked it in Mike's file cabinet. Not that she wanted to see the contents, but wondered if it contained any information that might help identify its creator. She'd been spending time at various libraries, reading computer magazines, and practicing commands on discs she'd created.

The near-blizzard had driven everyone inside, using the opportunity to catch up on overdue paperwork. The guys didn't work quietly—they chatted among themselves, comparing notes and sharing gossip with Betty. Even Mike took part in the chatter, but he avoided her desk unless he had a specific question.

Annie leaned back, stood to stretch, then wandered over to stare out the window. Mike joined her.

"It's pretty, isn't it?" she said.

"Until the soot covers it," he answered.

It took a moment for her to process, then she fought to maintain her composure. "That's Pittsburgh for you. Do you have time to look at a report?"

He nodded. "Of course. I'll meet you in my office."

She took her time gathering up some paperwork to make the meeting look business related. Which it was, but for different reasons. Annie walked into his office and closed the door. The office wasn't soundproofed, but the employees respected Mike enough to stay at their desks and not eavesdrop.

After handing him the stack of papers, Annie asked, "So, what's up? Is Mrs. Hansen upset we haven't given her an update?"

"She called, but not for that. Hansen asked her to go out with him tonight. He didn't say where, but told her to wear jeans."

"That could mean he's going to The Outlaw, but why would he take her?" Annie ran her fingers through her hair.

Mike shook his head. "I don't know. Use her for cover? Maybe he's actually trying to fix the marriage? She turned him down, anyway, because Wednesdays are her book club night, and she's in charge of the discussion for this one. She mentioned a lonesome dove, whatever that means."

"It's a popular book. A Western." Annie had heard two women talking about it in the library. "I haven't read it."

"Huh. Anyway, he told her he might stay home. He's done that a lot the last week or so. She said he has what she described as a new toy. A computer." One side of Mike's mouth curled.

"I want to examine it." Annie planted her hands on Mike's desk and leaned forward. "Can we break the rules and see if Owen can get me into the house?"

Mike leaned on the desk from his side so that his eyes were on the same level as hers. "What do you know about Owen's skills that I don't?"

She hated lying to Mike. "Just some chatter I heard when I spent time at Coulson's office."

He leaned in closer. "Do you want to continue to work for me? We don't break the law, no matter how hard it makes our jobs. Got it?"

Annie didn't back down. "Got it."

"Besides, I can't allow you to do anything that might compromise a police investigation." Mike straightened.

She copied his posture. "Understood."

He shook his head. "What am I going to do with you?"

"You're going to tell me what you want to do about Hansen tonight."

"Nothing. He's staying home. So am I."

"You're a liar." Annie said. "You're as invested in this case as I am. You won't risk an opportunity to nail this asshole."

"My gut is screaming this is a setup. I can't put you in danger." Mike removed his revolver from the shoulder harness slung on the back of his chair, and checked the safety was on.

"Then you need backup. That's me. Because you can't involve any of the guys. And it's my case. Right? Right, Mike?"

"I need someone who can be unemotional and stay professional. I don't doubt the professional part, but the emotional part. . ." He sighed. "Sorry, but I can't get past the fact that you're a woman."

She took several deep breaths and counted to ten. "We can have that argument later. In fact, I promise you we will have that discussion. But not now. Now you have to treat me like you'd treat any of the guys and figure out our plan of attack for tonight."

"There are no plans for tonight. I'm staying home, and so are you." Mike picked up some real paperwork, not the fake report Annie had brought in.

"You can't get rid of me that easy. Don't

forget, there are four men to help me. You might slip away from one, but not all of us.."

"Are you threatening me, Ms. McGregor?"

"Absolutely, Mr. Edwards."

They stared at each other.

He shook his head. "Have a seat, Annie."

No wig; Annie had styled her shoulder-length hair into a part on the left side. She'd carefully chosen her wardrobe from her limited selection and settled on a bland enough not-to-be remembered Steelers jersey from the back of the closet. She hid the revolver in her leg harness, because the shirt was too tight to cover it.

She examined the gun before pulling on her jeans. After her meeting with Mike, she'd taken it downstairs and fired a few practice rounds, blowing off steam. Mike had come down as she cleaned her weapon, and shot a few rounds of his own. They hadn't spoken since Simon had also been there, so Annie and Mike couldn't discuss the case.

Mike was right—Hansen might not even show up at The Outlaw. The plan was to get to the bar before him, and not follow him from his home. It was risky—he might go somewhere entirely different and they wouldn't know—but the ploy would give them a deeper cover.

As she walked to the convenience store a few blocks away, she mulled over the plan one more time, looking for any flaws. Mike had prepared for every contingency, including not picking her up at home. That way, he could identify if anyone followed her to the meeting.

Annie almost didn't recognize Mike as he knelt in front of a shelf of snacks. The Willie Nelson t-shirt was a size too big and hid his shoulder harness. He'd dyed his short hair black, and sported a hefty five o'clock shadow. She thought it suited him. But he was her boss; and this was strictly business.

"The car is out back and unlocked," he said, as if he were talking to himself. "No one followed you in."

She nodded as she picked up a bag of barbecue-flavored chips. "Back door?"

"Yep. You'll have to fight the stacks of pop bottles."

He stood, holding a package of red licorice, and moved to the refrigerated section. Nothing more needed to be said.

Annie took her chips to the checkout. "Are the restrooms open?" she asked the clerk.

He nodded as he rang up her purchase and handed her the change. "They're unlocked."

Easy. Now he wouldn't watch her as she headed to the back. She didn't stop at the restrooms, but navigated around the cases of cola and headed out the back door. Mike's rusty

Pinto was a short distance down the alley. She got in, checked the mirrors to see if anyone else was in sight, then waited.

But not for long. Annie was feeling the chill when Mike came around the corner of the store. He climbed in, tossed his bag of snacks into the back, and started the engine.

"Last chance to call it off," he said.

She'd been to The Outlaw enough times that it didn't hold any sense of trepidation. "Not a chance."

The Outlaw wasn't busy, and Annie worried she and Mike would be noticeable. Too many familiar faces meant the other patrons might recognize her, too. She hoped the change in hairdo and wardrobe would do the trick.

What it did was make it easy to see that Hansen wasn't there. None of his friends were there, either. Every time someone new walked in, Annie mentally checked their faces against the people she'd seen at the video store. None matched. The night might be a washout.

"The bartenders are going to have an easy night," Annie said as Mike set their beers on a table near the wall in the middle of the room. They sat next to each other, instead of across the table, to make it easier to have a conversation without being overheard.

"I'm guessing they're hoping business picks up once folks get done with supper. None of the local teams have games tonight, and fans will be bored staying home, flipping through channels," Mike said.

Normal people didn't know boring unless they'd spent a few nights watching lights flickering on and off in a home, waiting for a cheater to show up. "I haven't followed sports since high school. I'd rather spend my time reading."

"What do you read? I'm guessing historical fiction." Mike took a deep swig of his beer.

Annie sipped hers. "Biographies, mostly. And science-fiction. I tried reading Raymond Chandler, but it seemed unrealistic."

He chuckled. "And now?"

Neither Mike nor Annie had a string of sexual partners like Chandler's characters. All the guys were married, although Ric and his wife were talking divorce. "I'd have to reread them."

"Safe answer."

"What do you do in your spare time?" Annie asked as she studied the man sitting alone at the end of the bar. He looked familiar, but he wasn't one of the men who'd visited the video store.

He snorted. "What spare time?"

"That's what I figured." She jerked her

chin towards the bar. "Do you recognize that guy, by any chance? The one in the brown leather jacket?"

Mike glanced that direction. "No. Why?"

"He's watching us. But I can't catch him in the act."

"He's waiting for me to leave so he can take his shot at you," Mike chuckled.

She grinned. "Or you."

With a second quick glance, Mike shook his head. "He's not my type."

"Don't turn around, but look who's here," Annie said, leaning forward and touching Mike on the hand.

"Hansen?" he asked.

She nodded. "He's alone. Took a seat at the bar, but he might be just waiting for a drink. No one has approached him yet."

"It's too soon. Be patient."

"I know, I know." Annie lifted her beer to her lips but didn't drink. "Now that's interesting."

"What's that?"

"The dude at the end of the bar is checking out Hansen, just like he checked you out."

"Someone set him up with a blind date and he's been stood up?" Mike suggested with a grin.

"Or he's mixed up and came to the wrong bar."

"Is he wearing a wedding ring? That

opens up a whole new list of possibilities," Mike suggested.

"I can't see." Annie jerked her head towards the front. "One of Hansen's friends showed up."

"Noted. Only the two of them?"

"So far. He's got a drink, and they've moved to a table up front. If you lean back, you can see them without being obvious."

With his beer in his hand, Mike followed her advice. "I recognize him from your pics at the video store."

"One is a chance," Annie muttered.

"And two just walked in the door. He's not acknowledging either Hansen or number one. Looking everywhere but at them," Mike pointed out.

"Mr. Lonely Heart isn't paying attention to any of them. I guess he's given up on finding his soul mate."

Number one got up and headed towards the back. Annie assumed he was going to the restroom. Or outside, although she couldn't figure out a reason for it. It was too cold, and for her, still held the memory of that dead body. Mike started to stand, but Annie shook her head.

"Not now. Number three just walked in the door," she whispered.

"Hail, hail, the gang's all here?" he asked.

"Not quite, but I don't think I've ever seen them all in the same place at the same time." She leaned over to scratch her ankle and reassure herself her gun was where it belonged. Her stomach churned as if the baloney sandwich she'd eaten for supper suddenly disagreed with her.

"Are you okay?" Mike asked.

"Fine. The beer tastes off, that's all."

He didn't push her on it. "Two and three are talking and ignoring Hansen."

"They're blaming him for the lost disk and don't trust him anymore?" Annie suggested. "But still need something from him?"

"Makes sense. Let's watch and see what happens." Mike picked up his beer and settled in.

It would be a long night if nothing happened. Or all hell could break loose. And they were outnumbered.

Annie pretended to sip her beer and waited. For what, she wasn't sure. She bumped Mike's arm. "Did you notice that number one hasn't returned?"

"Yeah, I noticed. Hansen keeps looking that way. I'm about to go check on him."

She wasn't crazy about the idea, but didn't see a reason to object. "I'll watch your beer for you."

He nodded, stood, and wobbled his way back towards the restrooms in the perfect imitation of a man who'd had slightly too much to drink. Alarm bells rang when number two headed that direction, with no way to warn Mike.

But he was used to working alone, so he'd be fine.

Hansen went to the bar and talked to the bartender, getting another drink. Nothing unusual there. Instead of returning to his previous spot, he stopped to chat with number three. Still no cause for alarm.

Mike was taking too long. Or was her uneasiness slowing time to a crawl?

Then Hansen headed towards the back. But Annie had no chance to intercept him, because number three kept a close watch on Hansen. She wasn't skilled enough as an actress to pull off accidentally bumping into him.

Once he reached the back hallway, she lost track of him. Had he gone to the restroom or headed outside? Still no Mike.

Annie leaned over and this time, when she straightened, her gun nestled in her hand, covered by her sleeve. Left-handed, she raised her mug to her lips and pretended to drink before getting up. She leaned against the wall for a moment, as if finding her balance, then wound her way between tables and followed in Hansen's footsteps.

She paused outside the ladies' room; her left hand on the door, and listened. Loud voices didn't seem to be coming from the main bar or the men's bathroom. Annie cracked open the door to the alley and heard nothing more than sirens in the distance. That left what she'd assumed was a closet. The voices had fallen silent. Where was Mike?

To keep to her cover story, she had to go into the restroom. Not that she'd use it, she'd been in there before, and wouldn't risk her health. With a paper towel, Annie turned on the faucet and ran the water for a few seconds. It almost muffled the sound. Almost.

Chapter Twenty-Six

Annie had heard that sound before at the agency's gun range when Jorge had shown her the difference a silencer made. Despite the name, it wasn't silent, but muffled.

Mike didn't use a silencer.

She clicked off the safety on her gun and yanked open the bathroom door. She barely paused before tugging on the closet door. It wasn't a closet. It was an office. A small office, crowded by Hansen, the bartender, suspects one and two, and Mike slumped on the floor. Blood streamed from his shoulder, soaking his shirt and dripping onto the floor.

A gun dangled from the bartender's hand.

"Drop it," Annie commanded, her voice harsh with stress.

Still, the bartender didn't move his gun hand. "You can't take us all on."

"No, but I can take down two of you. Maybe three. You're first. My choice for the second one." Annie's aim wavered as her gaze swept the room.

Number one took half a step towards her. Calmly, as if she was at target practice, Annie swung the gun, aimed for center mass, and squeezed the trigger.

She didn't wait for a reaction. Whipping

her weapon back, she pointed it at the bartender. "One," she counted.

Immediately, the bartender dropped his gun and raised his hands. She'd expected more of a fight.

A deep voice behind her said "I've got your back. I'm Detective Strait. Help is on the way. Is Mike okay?"

"I don't know. I've been preoccupied. But he hasn't said a word. I'm worried." She glanced over her shoulder. It was Mr. Lonely Heart. Mike had betrayed her trust again.

"You a cop? Arrest her," Hansen screamed. "She's crazy. She shot both these guys and swore she'd pin it on us."

"Tell it to the judge. Now, turn around and put your hands on the wall. All of you," Strait barked.

Sirens wailed outside. The rest was up to the authorities.

It was mid-afternoon the next day before Annie stepped out of the local precinct. The way they treated her switched from a suspect to more of a consultant after an hour. She'd walked the newly created task force of detectives and street cops through her investigation, and explained what the discs they found on each of the suspects were. The local guys didn't have computer set-ups to view the contents, and the discs were sent off to experts at police headquarters. Annie was both relieved and dismayed that she was cut out of that part of the investigation. She would have liked to show off her minor expertise, but dreaded seeing the results.

Of course, she'd have nothing to do with questioning of the suspects, the flurry of warrants, or the coordination of raids to serve those warrants, including one for the video shop. Her part of the story was over. At least until the trials, when she'd have to serve as a witness.

That was the official reasons she received only limited updates. But she suspected the cops didn't want to share the glory of the bust. Strait kept her up-to-date about Mike's condition. He'd been whisked into surgery immediately after the ambulance arrived at the hospital. Strait contacted Betty and Jorge, so Mike had support once he regained consciousness.

Although Annie snatched a few cat naps between interviews, she was exhausted. She needed sleep before visiting Mike.. She looked like crap, and didn't want him to worry about her. That meant calling a taxi to take her home.

Or not. "Need a ride?" Coulson asked, jumping out of his car parked at the curb.

"Where'd you come from?' she asked, too tired to react.

"News gets around. Good work, Annie."

"How much do you know?"

He grinned. "Not as much as I pretend. My normal contacts aren't talking. That means it's something huge. Then there's the rumor about you saving Mike's life. What gives, Annie?"

He held open the passenger side door, and she slid in.

"I'm sworn to secrecy." She fastened her seatbelt and leaned back, closing her eyes before Coulson even shut the door.

"Long day?" he asked

"Long night." Annie blinked, trying to stay awake.

It didn't work.

She woke up enough for Coulson to walk her upstairs to her apartment. And tuck her into her bed. Alone.

When Annie got to the hospital, visitors' hours were almost over. The cop standing guard looked through a paper file, nodded, and let her pass. The faint odor of bitter soap assailed her nose as her eyes adjusted to see Mike in the bed in the darkened room, sleeping.

She sat in the most uncomfortable chair in the room to keep herself awake. The cop at the door bothered her—was there a threat to

Mike's life? Or were the police making sure that no one tried to corrupt his memory?

There were a few magazines scattered around the room, and Annie chose a *People* magazine with Dan Russell on the cover. If nothing else, reading about his latest exploits would provide a distraction.

She put down the magazine when Mike groaned and rolled to his side. "Hello. Mike."

"Annie?" His eyes popped open. "You're here."

"Sorry, I came as soon as I could." She stood and moved to make it easier for him to see her.

"Where have you been?" Mike's voice rasped.

Annie put her hand on top of his, the one without the miles of tubes attached. "Spending too much time with your friend, Detective Strait, as he pulled information from my brain that I'd forgotten."

He tried to laugh, but it came out as a cough. Annie picked up the nearby water container and held the straw to Mike's lips. He sucked at it greedily. "What did you tell him?"

"Them. Strait decided it was bigger than he could handle by himself. I lost track of how many cops ended up part of the investigation. There were mutters of bringing in the FBI."

"That's why they haven't talked to me yet," he said, his voice just above a whisper.

Was he wearing out already? No one had revealed just how bad his injury was. "Sounds right. I'm under strict orders not to discuss the case with anyone, including you."

His eyes closed, but his breathing was uneven, so Annie didn't think he was asleep. He'd talk when he had the strength to. She sat and picked up the magazine again, flipping back to where she'd left off.

She didn't get more than one page read before he spoke again.

"You," Mike said. "You saved my life."

Annie hadn't thought of it that way.

"I knew when you came in," he croaked. "An avenging angel, come to my rescue."

"Why did they shoot you? They must have dealt with drunks getting in their way before. Is that what happened to Rimer? The dead man I found in the alley?"

After knocking, a nurse strode into the room to check Mike's vitals. Annie stood in the corner and stayed out of the way. By the time the nurse completed her work, Mike seemed to be asleep. Annie waited for a few minutes so he wouldn't be alone.

But even sitting in the uncomfortable chair, the day caught up with her. A different nurse woke her a few hours later. Noiselessly, Annie left the room and headed home.

"I've been railroaded," Annie muttered as she sat in Mike's chair and stared at his computer screen.

Betty and Jorge had presented it to her as a done deal. While Mike was out for two weeks or more, someone had to be in charge. Since Annie knew the books, and had to be off the streets so the cops could reach her about the ongoing investigation, they decided she was the perfect candidate.

She shouldn't be here. She should be at the hospital, while Mike underwent a second surgery. Instead, everyone was looking to her to keep the business running. Jorge and Denny were at the hospital, so Mike wasn't alone.

She turned on the computer, and while waiting for it to load, tackled the stack of messages that Betty had put in Mike's "in" box, sorting them by urgency. Several were "get well soon" wishes, and Annie wondered who had leaked the information about Mike's injury. The bust hadn't made the news.

There was one from Coulson, offering his assistance in whatever form was needed. It was a nice professional courtesy, but Annie recognized Coulson meant it.

The five messages from Leona Hansen made Annie cross her arms on Mike's desk and lay her head on top of them. There was so much she couldn't tell their client. Had the cops even served a warrant on the home yet? But Leona deserved to be told her husband was alive.

She looked up at a knock on the door.

"You have a visitor, Ms. McGregor," Betty said.

So, this was official business. Annie wondered which department had bothered to send someone to her, rather than summoning her to them. The man hovering around Betty's desk was dressed in a black suit, which didn't read like a normal Pittsburgh cop.

Annie didn't need this. She didn't like this part of Mike's job. There was a lot of Mike's job she didn't like.

Betty mouthed "FBI."

There had been muttering about bringing in the big guns. "Send him in. And bring me some coffee, please?" she added with a wink.

It was a tactic Mike used. If things got too tense during a meeting with a client, he'd push the intercom button on the telephone but not say anything, and soon Betty would magically appear with a fresh cup of black coffee. Other times, he fetched his own.

Betty nodded. She knew the drill.

The man stood at the door to the office and looked around, as if he was trying to match Annie to the clearly masculine surroundings. She took the moment to analyze him. Average height, shoulders that strained the seams of his jacket, short hair that had grayed too early. The bags under his eyes gave every indication that he was operating without enough sleep. Annie broke her own rule and punched the intercom button.

"Two cups of coffee," she said. "Black, Agent?"

He nodded.

She stood and held out her hand. "C.T. McGregor."

"Special Agent Reuben Foster." He grasped her hand with the perfect amount of firmness. Not too hard, not too soft. "I apologize, but I was told Mr. Mike Edwards ran the agency."

"Your sources neglected to tell you he is still hospitalized. The fools out there," and she indicated the main room with a tip of her head, "voted me most likely to not piss anyone off in his absence. Have a seat and tell me why you're here."

Foster chuckled. "I appreciate your honesty. As you may have guessed, I'm assigned to the Striker case."

Annie scrunched her eyebrows. "I'm not familiar with it. Or does it have a different name?"

Betty came in with the coffees and set them on the desk. "Anything else?"

"No, thanks. But hang close, in case I need you."

Betty closed the door behind her.

"Now, what case are we talking about?" Annie asked.

"The owner of The Outlaw is Jerry Striker. The bartender involved is his nephew, Bart

Striker. For simplicity's sake, we're using the name for the overall investigation."

That made sense. Annie picked up her coffee. "In that case, you know my involvement. I've shared what I know with the police. What did they miss?"

"When Mr. Edwards reached out to Detective Strait, he didn't reveal all the details of your agency's involvement. I'm looking for the missing pieces."

"This was my case within the agency. I can assist you." She steeled herself for the conversation with a deep swallow of the coffee. Betty had made it strong.

Foster copied her activity. "There was mention of the agency having information that ties the suspects to illegal activity that isn't admissible."

"Let's not pussyfoot around, Special Agent. I came across evidence of child porn." She opened Mike's top drawer and retrieved a key, then opened his locked file cabinet. She took out a manila envelope and placed it on the desk.

Her voice quavered as she continued. "My fingerprints are all over the disk. I thought I'd bumped into stolen business information or something. I didn't know anything like this existed."

"Let's clarify. You're talking a computer floppy disk?" Foster asked as he picked up the envelope.

She swallowed back the bile that rose. "Yes. The images are crude, in more than one meaning of the word. Think of what a picture looks like when it's been faxed, and that fax is faxed again, and repeat about twenty times."

"I've heard rumors of such a thing, but haven't seen it in person." He opened the top of the envelope almost reverently. "Do you have gloves or tissue available?"

Mike always kept a box of tissue on his bookshelf in case a client got emotional. Annie passed the container to the FBI man. He took one out and used it to remove the disk from the envelope. "It doesn't look like much, but if you described the contents correctly, this could become a historical exhibit in the Agency archives."

"I can't connect it directly to any of the suspects," Annie warned. "But you might find similar files on Hansen's computer. Mike wouldn't allow me to try to access it."

Foster looked at his watch. "They should be serving that warrant any time now. The wife of one of the suspects was your client, correct?"

She nodded. "Leona Hansen. She's convinced Bobby Hansen is cheating based on his erratic spending, but we found no proof of it."

"If he's involved in the situation, we'll find it. Home movies, VHS tapes, even photo albums. We'll have to get one of our geeks to check the computer."

"I wish I could be there. Not that I want to see more files, but I'd like to watch how your experts conduct the search." The articles Annie had read didn't give her enough details.

"Are you a nerd, Ms. McGregor?" Foster grinned. "I might be able to arrange it."

She'd heard the term before, usually as an insult, but never thought it applied to her. She liked it.

"Not many people would know the difference between a computer disk and garbage," he continued. "It's fortunate you did. That's why they pulled me away from my desk in DC to work this case. You say the disk came from The Outlaw. How did you get your hands on it?"

She stood and planted both hands on Mike's desk. "This is where you flash your badge at me, toss a business card on the desk, and look aggressive so the guys don't think I'm a total pushover."

Foster blinked, grinned, and shoved his chair back so hard its legs screeched against the floor. He stood, pushed his jacket back to reveal the badge on his belt, and scowled so deeply that lines formed on his forehead. "Is this what you want?"

"Absolutely." Annie poked a finger into his chest. "An acquaintance found it wrapped in plastic and taped to the inside of the toilet tank in the men's room."

He nudged her finger aside. "An

acquaintance, huh? Since we don't know who the disk was meant for, we can't use it as evidence, so I'll let that slide. Can we use this computer to see what we have?"

Annie felt the blood drain from her face and she sat down heavily in Mike's chair, then slumped to put her head to her knees.

"This isn't part of the act, is it?" Foster asked, as he came around the desk and crouched beside her. "Are you all right?"

"There were only eight grainy pictures." Annie whispered. "But I see them in my nightmares every night. What kind of grown man would do that to a kid? An eight or nine-year-old, if I had to guess."

Betty barged into the office. "Are you okay, Annie? What did you do to her, Agent? It's not about Mike, is it?"

"Not Mr. Edwards. Water. Now." Foster ordered. "Take deep breaths, Ms. McGregor. In and hold. Exhale. In. Slowly."

By the time Betty returned, Annie had regained her composure. She took the offered glass and chugged down half of the water.

"I'm fine now, Betty. What has Mike told you about my case?" Annie asked.

"Only that it's bad, and I should keep my nose out of it."

Annie nodded. Betty got the hint and left.

"That's why we're a special task force," Foster said. "We never get immune to what we find, but I've learned to compartmentalize it. I'll look at the disk later."

"I appreciate that."

Foster stood and returned to his chair. "We'll get these guys. And women, too."

She took another gulp of the water. "Is there anything else, Agent?"

"I still owe you a business card." Foster pulled a small leather case out of his suit coat pocket, retrieved a card, and laid it on the desk. "Annie?"

With a shrug, she told him. "My given name is Cheyenne. I go by C.T. for professional reasons. Makes people take me more seriously."

"Because as a woman in this field, they don't." He grinned. "My wife tells me about it all the time. She's also an agent, but with a different specialty."

Annie had a small stack of her business cards on the corner of Mike's desk, and she slid one over to Foster. "Now we're even. But can you answer one question?"

"Sure. Ask, but I won't promise you an answer."

That was fair. She took a moment to gather her courage. "The man I shot. Is he alive? The local law enforcement guys wouldn't tell me."

"I don't know specifics," Foster said. "But there's no mention in the reports about anyone dying."

He stood and extended his hand. "Now

for the formal part. The department thanks you for your assistance in this matter. If we need anything else, we'll be in touch."

She accepted the proffered hand. "You know where to find me. Have a good day, Special Agent."

Chapter Twenty-Seven

Annie heard the front door open and looked up. It was late, and she wasn't expecting customers. Had Mike disobeyed doctor's orders and come into the office?

She'd been reviewing Jorge's latest report with a critical eye. He was a great investigator but she'd redone this one three times. She wanted perfection before presenting it to Mike. To keep him out of the office during his recovery, they'd give him paperwork to review daily. It was an excuse to check up on him. Today was her turn.

Annie put down the paperwork and waited for Betty's scolding greeting. It didn't come. In fact, the rest of the office was dark, except one corner where Simon normally sat. She didn't worry about being alone, not with her revolver in its holster slunk over the back of the chair, but how late was it?

"Ms. McGregor?" a familiar voice called. Not Mike.

"In here," she responded. "Mr. Edwards' office, Detective Myers."

"You should lock the door when you're here alone," he said as he entered.

"I should." Annie rolled her eyes. "But I'm rarely alone. The guys have a habit of making sure one of them is around when I am here. I guess they messed up today. Got their wires crossed."

Myers chuckled. "This isn't a high-crime area. And you have a reputation that would scare most intruders."

Was that a compliment or an insult? "I'd offer you coffee, but Betty empties and turns off the pot when she leaves. Why are you here, Detective?"

"To request a favor. And information. About computers. I get the gist of what they do, but am vague on the details."

Annie nodded. "I've been spending my spare time learning more about them, and still, there's so much I don't understand. Is there something specific you're wondering about?"

"I wasn't involved in the Striker case, but the entire office is talking about it." He scrunched his mouth. "I keep hearing the words 'floppy disk' and 'sneaker net'. What do they mean?"

"First one is easy." Annie chose a disk from Mike's desk and held it up. "This is a floppy disk. It's storage. I can save things from the computer to this. It's like taking a paper file and running it through the copy machine. Now you have two copies. One on the computer, one on here."

"And sneaker net?"

She grinned and waved the disk in the air.

"I can take this, walk over to my computer, pop it in the right slot, and see the information that I composed here. The people who created the system have a reputation for wearing tennis shoes, so sneaker net or network. Like you have a network of informants."

"Huh." Myers reached into his coat pocket and pulled out a folded piece of paper. He set it on the desk, and unfolded it to reveal a disk, a twin to what Annie held. "So that's a floppy disk."

Her gut told her this was important. Annie leaned forward. "Yes. Where did it come from?"

"The personal effects of Harold Rimer." The detective held her eyes with a long stare.

He continued. "I can't shake the feeling that his case and the current one are connected. I reviewed my report and found nothing. Then I remembered the odd bit of plastic that was recovered, and paid a visit to the evidence locker. Not that he'd had much other than his clothes. Just his beat-up wallet and a few coins. And this. Can you tell me what is on it?"

She reached for it, then pulled her hand back. "Yes, I could, but no, I won't. I don't want to change or destroy potential evidence. This needs to go to Special Agent Foster."

"You've come to the same conclusion as I did." Myers re-wrapped the disk in its makeshift container.

"That Rimer was murdered because he

either stole that disk from one of the suspects or he was a runner for them and demanded more money." Annie closed her eyes, pushing back the memory of Rimer in the alley. The blood, the stench, the expression of horror on Rimer's face.

"Or any variety of those." Myers put the disk back in his pocket and stood. "The suspects may not rat each other out, but it'll be fun making them sweat when they realize what we have. The warrants produced a wealth of evidence. We might push for conspiracy. There are years of hard time in the future for them."

Annie followed him to the front door, prepared to lock it behind him. He turned at the last minute.

A classic Columbo move, Annie thought. What did Myers plan to spring on her?

"Sister Justice," he said, shaking his head. "That's a good one. Has she retired? Or did she show up at The Outlaw?"

"That was me. All me. Sister Justice was a rumor," Annie said. "She never really existed."

Annie waited for the detective to leave the parking lot before gathering up paperwork to take to Mike. She'd left a few minor errors in each report. That way, Mike would feel needed when he found them.

Annie anticipated that Mike's first day back would be chaos, so she isolated herself in the basement, firing round after round. Besides, she didn't think Mike would venture down so soon and the privacy would give her more time to think.

She headed upstairs to get coffee an hour after Mike's arrival, hoping things would have settled down. Jorge should be out on an insurance case. Ric should be getting some sleep, because he'd had a late night following a cheater. Simon and Denny were doing side work for Coulson, although that included a lot of phone calls. Annie was the only one without an assignment. With Mike back in the office, she'd be relegated to being no more than a secretary. She'd gotten used to being in charge, and it would be hard to be demoted to the bottom of the heap.

But everyone was still there. Annie ignored them as she headed to her desk. She didn't want to talk to anyone.

Mike had left a small stack of paperwork for her, the corrections to the last round of reports she'd given him. She'd made the corrections already, but she fired up her computer, anyway. She pretended to work, while she actually tested a new tip she'd come across in a computer tech magazine.

She heard his footsteps first, even over the clacking of her keyboard, then the rich, forest-like scent of his aftershave tickled her nose. Annie tore her attention from her computer screen. "Good morning, Mike. Welcome back."

"Ms. McGregor. In my office. Now," he snarled, a wolf harassing its prey.

Annie didn't ask questions. With the eyes of her coworkers on her, she stood and trailed him to his lair. Once inside, she closed the door and waited for him to speak.

A sole string of Christmas lights hung around the door by Betty's desk reflected in Mike's darkened computer screen. He took his time, focusing his stare on her, as if he could bore into her soul and extract every secret she held. She stood, spine straight, staring back, not giving an inch. Then he picked up a piece of paper from his desk.

"What is this, Ms. McGregor?" He waved it in the air with his good arm.

She didn't need to hold it to know what it was. Her resignation letter. "I'm sorry, Mike," she said. "You know I've been working in here, but I didn't mean to leave this for you to find."

"Why?" The single word echoed in the small office.

Annie licked her lips, formulating her answer, before speaking. "You haven't paid yourself for the past two months. The bills for the hospital are coming in and although you might recoup that money in a civil suit, it will take years. There are too many unpaid invoices. In the file cabinet behind you, in the third drawer, in a file marked 'Oldgrew,' is an application for a business loan from Mellon Bank. I'm a private investigator. I put together the pieces."

"And your conclusion?"

"I'm the newest and least productive employee in terms of bringing in revenue. You can't afford to keep paying me, but don't want to fire me." Annie snatched the paper from Mike's hand. "So, I'm taking that decision out of your hands."

Mike's mouth gaped open, but no words tumbled out. His chair creaked as he sat.

"I built this agency from scratch and my savings. I've never borrowed money to run it. But I can't stop the constant money drain without more customers.

"Then I heard rumors that the Oldgrew agency was closing. If I buy the company, I might get enough business to keep going."

"I guessed that. I did some research of my own. That agency has a shady reputation, and their investigators are lazy and incompetent. You don't want to besmirch your reputation by associating with them."

"So, what am I going to do?" he asked. "I don't want to fire you. You have great potential as an investigator. None of the guys have busted a porn ring. Or," he paused, "saved my life."

Annie had come prepared. "I have a proposal. You need to expand into a new field. Computer security. With me in charge. We can start off by hiring the top of the class over at Carnegie Mellon for short-term jobs and later develop a full-time staff. Like Coulson does with Owen and others. I already have a reputation with the police and FBI because of the Striker case, and we can build on that."

"I can't imagine there's enough call to create a business around that."

"Not now. And it's a risk, but this is a chance to be on the ground floor of a new field. If the bad guys are using computers, there's going to be a need for someone the good guys can turn to. Why not us?"

Mike shook his head. "Before you started working for me, I could barely turn a computer on. How can I run an agency dealing with the damn things?"

"And that's the other reason I have to resign. To do this right, I have to be in charge of the computer part while you remain in charge of the PI side of the business. I have to be your partner, not your employee. That doesn't mean I can't still do jobs with you, or that you can't assign the guys to help me out." She'd tried to cover all the angles in her plans and hoped she was wearing down Mike's resistance.

"If it's such a good idea, why don't you do it on your own, instead of tying yourself down to me, who's failed at both being a cop and running a PI firm?"

"Are you feeling sorry for yourself, Mr. Edwards?"

He shook his head. "No, I'm dealing with the reality that I messed up that night at the Outlaw. I overestimated my ability to get out of a rough situation, and damnit, I could have gotten you killed! And yet, you still want to be connected to me—my agency."

"Think about it. How much resistance there is to the fact that I'm a woman in a field dominated by men." Annie cocked her head. "Consider how people will react to a woman in charge of a staff of college-age men working with computers. Now think about having The Edwards Agency as the lead company and the difference it makes."

"I can't dispute that. You've put a lot of thought into this." Mike shook his head. "Manipulating me when I'm down."

"You approached me," Annie reminded him.

"I did. I've been outmaneuvered again."

"If nothing else, I promise to keep you on your toes. You'll need to have the company lawyer look over the paperwork, of course. The lawyer I talked to says it isn't the most complicated setup he's ever handled, but I want to protect your ownership of the agency."

"Why me?" Mike asked. "Why not

Coulson?"

"Because you trust me and treat me as an equal. Coulson will always see me first as a potential romantic interest. Even if I'm the expert on computers, he'd want to be in charge."

"You've got him figured out." Mike adjusted his sling. "How about me?"

He was treading in dangerous territory. "I plead the fifth," Annie laughed.

Mike tented his fingers. It looked awkward with his sling. "Partners, huh? And I suppose you want to rename the agency to Edwards and McGregor?"

She'd thought about it, but didn't want to immortalize Ian's name. "No. How about The Edwards Agency, Private Investigations and Computer Security? It's not too long, is it?"

"We'll have to work on it. If," and he held up his good hand in a stop signal, "If I decide to accept your offer."

She guessed that the money for the renovations came from Mike's personal funds. The wooden framing for her office space was hammered into place before the lawyers completed their negotiations. By the time the walls went up, Annie had her first client, courtesy of a referral from Mother Hilary. With the help of Andreas, the president of the computer club at the university, they'd closed the case in three days.

She sat behind her computer, but stared aimlessly into space when Mike walked in.

"What are you working on?" he asked.

She grinned and shook her head. "You caught me daydreaming. Now I'm sitting here in my own office, I'm planning for things I want."

He'd already equipped her office with two used file cabinets and a brand-new desk. A white cowboy hat sat on top of one of the file cabinets. Betty had placed a miniature vase of artificial purple and yellow flowers on the corner of the desk, a 'housewarming' gift. "What else do you need?"

"Bookshelves." She waved her hand towards one wall. "There are lots of computer reference books and manuals I want to buy. A coat rack."

He came around the desk and put his hands on her shoulders. Both hands. He only wore his sling occasionally these days. She didn't object.

"Anything else?" he asked.

"A whiteboard for that wall." Annie pointed to her right.

Mike laughed. "What's that?"

"Think of a blackboard, only white. And you use things like magic markers to write on it, and the ink can be erased. Andreas told me about them. I guess they are all the rage in the tech world."

"Speaking of him, I have his paycheck." Mike pulled an envelope from his pocket and laid it on her desk. "Kelly Landrow, the owner of the business, paid his invoice immediately. What magic did you work?"

"It was easy once Mr. Landrow gave his bookkeeper the day off and we got full access to his computer. I spotted the problems in his accounting report right away. The numbers didn't add up. Nothing huge, and most of the discrepancies could be excused as typos.

"While I was working on the accounting spreadsheet, Andreas analyzed the computer itself. He found records of a second copy of the financial info, with minor differences." Annie swiveled her chair around to look at Mike. "We found a disk hidden in the bottom drawer of his desk. You can guess the rest."

He nodded. "The bookkeeper was skimming off the top. Not enough to shut down the business, but he was padding his pockets."

"Exactly. The hard part is that it's a family run business, and his bookkeeper is his brother-in-law. Landrow figures that the money we will save him long term makes us the best investment he's ever made. Plus, he got to fire the guy, who he's never liked."

"I only understand about half of what you do, but you've proven it works." Mike walked around to the front of her desk. "There's one more thing you're missing."

She narrowed her eyes, puzzled. "What?"

He grinned, walked out the doorway, reached down, and picked up a small object. He returned and placed it on her desk. "Here you go.".

Annie picked up the narrow box, cocked her head, and looked up at Mike. His expression didn't change as she lifted the lid and the tissue paper inside to uncover a black metal strip. She removed it and flipped it over.

It was a nameplate, engraved with gold lettering.

C.T. McGregor
Edwards Investigations

Mike took it from her hands and placed it on her desk. "Welcome to the agency, partner."

The End
(for now)

Acknowledgments

As always, thanks go to K.M. Guth, for her cover design and other graphic assistance. It was great fun working with her to fine tune the cover's final design.

To Cornelia Amiri, for her constant encouragement.

And to Horus Copyedit and Proofreading, for catching all those little things I missed.

Note To The Reader:

Thank you for reading Edwards Investigations: The Rimer Files. This story was first written over a decade ago, before I published my first book, Wolves' Pawn. Pack then, it was called The Edwards Agency. But as much as I loved the tale, I knew it wasn't "right." I picked at it over the years, trying to figure out what was wrong with it, and not coming up with an answer.

After finishing the Harmony Duprie series, I was ready to take another stab at it. Then Jake Hennessey got in the way, and I put it off again. But all that time, the story was rumbling around in the back of my head, and I figured out what it wanted. It took me almost two years to get the words into the right form and it bears little resemblance to the original version. I claim the story is a tribute to the first draft, not a rewrite. Almost everything has changed, except for Annie and Mike.

I hope you have grown to love them as much as I do. Yes, I plan to wrote more book in this series. I can't tell you how soon, but I pray the next one doesn't take as long as this one!

P.J. MacLayne

Contact

P.J. MacLayne can be reached at:
Website: https://pjmaclayne.com
Facebook https://facebook.com/pjmaclayne
Twitter https://twitter.com/pjmaclayne
Amazon http://www.amazon.com/P.J.-MacLayne/e/B00HVE8WZI
BookBub https://www.bookbub.com/profile/p-j-maclayne
Newsletter http://eepurl.com/cL73Cz

Other books by P.J. MacLayne

A Harmony Duprie Companion Story

The Fall of Jake Hennessey

Jake Hennessey deals in selling fine jewelry of an illegal nature. The thrill of getting away with it is his addiction. When he hears a rumor about a rare old book in the personal collection of a small-town librarian, he gets the urge to try a new game.

After all, even jewel thieves get bored.

But the librarian, Harmony Duprie, isn't what he expected and the challenge becomes serious business.

In order to win, Jake's going to have to play by a new set of rules—and make them up as he goes along—because this time, he's playing for the rest of his life.

Books in the

Harmony Duprie Mysteries Series

The Marquesa's Necklace

Harmony Duprie enjoyed her life in the quiet little town of Oak Grove—until her arrest for drug trafficking. Now she has to figure out who is behind the sinister incidents plaguing her, and why.

Her Ladyship's Ring

Harmony Duprie is back, and so is trouble in Oak Grove.

Her ex-boyfriend Jake is out of prison and a suspect in a murder. Can Harmony clear Jake's name and solve the mystery of her own heart?

The Baron's Cufflinks

What starts as Girl's Night Out ends in murder, and Harmony Duprie is a suspect.

She's innocent, of course, but with no alibi, the sheriff's department won't remove her from the list of suspects. But caution isn't Harmony's middle name and she plunges head first into danger to defend her honor.

The Contessa's Brooch

A firebug is stalking Oak Grove and internet researcher Harmony Duprie is on the case. It starts as a simple data analysis project for Police Chief Sorenson, but things get personal when the house she renovated is targeted.

The arsonist is in it for the glory, posting videos of his exploits on social media. Can Eli, Lando and Scotty, Harmony's favorite computer hackers, help her track down the pyromaniac before someone gets hurt? Or, worse yet, killed?

The Samurai's Inro

Harmony Duprie has it made. Or so she thinks.

New job.

New routine.

A quiet life in the quiet little town of Oak Grove.

Oh, and Eli.

But trouble has a long memory and it's playing a deadly game.

The Ranger's Dog Tags

It isn't the first time Eli Hennessey has disappeared. Is it the last?

The Rise of Jack Hennessey

A Harmony Duprie Companion Story

For 22 years, semi-retired jewel thief Jake Hennessey honored his promise to stay away from Harmony Duprie. He has no plans to change that...

until Special Agent Doan Houck saunters into Jake's bar, claiming Harmony's life is in danger.

Books in The Free Wolves Series

Wolves' Pawn

Book 1

Dot McKenzie is a lone wolf-shifter on the run. Can she survive when she becomes a pawn in a pack leader's deadly game?

Wolves' Knight

Book 2

Tasha Roeper knows what it means to protect your own. Torn between tradition and a changing world, will Tasha risk everything to save a friend—including her own life—when old enemies arise?

Wolves' Gambit

Book 3

Free Wolf Lori Grenville has made it her life's mission to help unhappy shifters escape from overbearing alphas and dangerous situations. She hasn't failed in a mission yet. This one may be the exception.